BEAUTY IN LINGERIE

Lingerie #2

PENELOPE SKY

Hartwick Publishing

Copyright © 2018 by Penelope Sky

All rights reserved.

No part of this book may be reproduced in any form or by any electronic or mechanical means, including information storage and retrieval systems, without written permission from the author, except for the use of brief quotations in a book review.

Contents

1. Sapphire 1
2. Conway 17
3. Sapphire 49
4. Conway 83
5. Sapphire 117
6. Conway 163
7. Sapphire 203
8. Conway 227
9. Sapphire 261
10. Conway 295
11. Sapphire 311

Also by Penelope Sky 319

1

Sapphire

Conway was gone all day at work. He went to Milan for a meeting with his assistant, Nicole. I knew how devoted he was to his work, so I didn't expect to see him until dinnertime. So I spent my time at the stables.

There were only six horses, but each one required extensive work. I started cleaning the stables, raking up their feces, and changing the hay. Sometimes their troughs would get dirty, and they needed to be scrubbed before they were refilled with water.

Marco appeared in the doorway to the stall. "Sapphire, you don't need to do that. That's my job."

"I don't mind." I held the hose over the now clean trough and filled it with water.

"A pretty lady like you shouldn't be getting her hands so dirty."

Conway already made me feel that way. He wanted to treat me like the possession he viewed me as. "I disagree. I think a real lady gets her hands dirty like a man."

He chuckled. "Well said, darling."

I walked out of the stall and then guided Aptos back inside, the brown mare with a gentle soul. I placed her inside and shut the door, but she poked her head out to look at me. I rubbed her on the snout. "Good girl."

I walked to the next stable, where Carbine was housed. The second the black horse saw me, he turned away, giving me his backside instead of his face. I'd made a connection with all of the horses, but this one was important to click with. He was angry all the time, showcasing a constantly irritated attitude.

"Not this one," Marco said. "Let me handle him."

"I can do it." I grabbed the bridle and the reins.

Marco barricaded the door with his size. "I enjoy having you around here, and if you get hurt, Conway won't allow it anymore. So I have to keep you safe—for my own self-interest. Just leave Carbine to me. He's a very aggressive horse."

Since he said it so sweetly, I let it go. "Alright, Marco. I'll take care of Lady, then."

"Excellent call."

At the end of the day, I left my clothes in a special hamper that Dante had instructed me to use. My shoes and jeans were covered with a mixture of horse shit, wet hay, and dust. He didn't want any of that touching anything else in the mansion.

I took a long shower and scrubbed all the dirt off my body. My hair was caked with oil and sweat, and my fingernails were packed with dirt and grime. I rinsed everything away before I stepped out of the shower and wrapped my body in a towel.

My bedroom was made for a princess, so I didn't mind being in there. It never had felt like a prison cell since the day I arrived. I had my own space, even a living room where I could read and watch whatever I wanted on TV. Conway had a special program so I could watch American networks because everything else was in Italian.

Even though I should probably learn the language.

I wasn't going anywhere anytime soon.

I suspected Conway would never let me go, and if he did, I would be much older.

In light of my position, I should be grateful. But a part of me always wondered how my life would have been if none of this had happened. What if I'd stayed in school and finished my education? What if my brother hadn't gotten mixed up with the wrong people? What if I weren't living in Conway's mansion? Would I have fallen in love with my soul mate and had a family?

Now, I would never know.

It made me sad, so I tried not to think about it.

My thoughts turned to Knuckles, thinking about what Conway had said about him the other day. Knuckles was angry that Conway had outbid him, probably because he lost me and took a blow to his pride.

I never wanted to be underneath that man. I never wanted him to touch me. I never wanted him to look at me.

I would much rather be with Conway.

The door to my bedroom opened, and Conway appeared. He was in a three-piece suit, navy blue and crisp. Instead of greeting me with a smile or even a hello, his green eyes focused on me venomously. It wasn't clear whether he was pleased or pissed. It was a storm of intensity, a warning of an attack.

I stood in my towel with damp hair, unsure if I should be afraid or not.

Then he marched toward me, backing me up into the wall. He snatched my towel and yanked it off before he pressed his body into mine. His hand gripped my neck forcefully, and he crushed his mouth to mine.

Then he kissed me like he hadn't seen me in weeks.

With my tits pressed against his chest and my body pinned in place, I kissed him back. My passion ignited the second I felt his flames. My arms circled his neck, and my fingers dug into his hair as I breathed with him. My nipples chafed against his jacket, so I peeled it off his body.

It fell to the floor with a quiet thud.

The tie came next, coming loose and falling off his body.

None of this made any sense. I shouldn't want to kiss him, no matter how attracted I was to him. I shouldn't feel indebted to him for protecting me, not when he bought me in the first place. But my life was no longer normal, and it didn't change the fact that I wanted him. He took my virginity, and now he would always have a piece of me.

I unbuttoned his collared shirt, starting from the top and moving to the bottom as our kiss continued. He breathed into me deeply, his kiss as ferocious as it was in the beginning. He squeezed my tits and rubbed his thumbs over my nipples.

I pushed the shirt over his shoulder, finally revealing his perfect body.

That's when I saw it—the lipstick on his neck.

A jolt of jealousy rampaged through my body, so sudden I didn't even feel it begin. The idea of a woman running her lips over his body while I was shoveling shit in his stables pissed me off. Maybe I was just a possession, but I didn't expect to share him. He couldn't take my virginity, fuck me without a condom, and then screw one of his models during the workday.

I shoved him hard in the chest. "That's not how this is going to work, asshole."

He stumbled back, his expression so blank he clearly had no idea what was going on. He took a few more steps back then stopped, all the muscles in his body tight from the way he tensed. His temper ran rampant through his body, his physique projecting his emotions so easily. He was so cut it didn't seem real.

"You can have me, but don't expect me to turn the other way while you fuck your models at work. I'm not catching anything, so if that's how this is going to be, then you're wearing a condom." I wasn't sure if a condom would even satisfy me. He took my virginity and did it as romantically as possible—because he knew that was how I wanted it. Maybe I'd let my guard down and assumed more of him than I should. He never said we were exclusive, but if he was bedding me every night, why would he want anyone else?

He lowered his hands to his sides, his eyebrows furrowed in irritation. "Where is this coming from?"

I pointed at my neck. "Make sure you wipe off your lipstick marks before you come home, *honey*." I felt like a poor wife waiting for her husband to come home, only to find out he was getting his kicks elsewhere.

He rubbed his palm along his neck then stared at his hand, inspecting the lipstick mark. His eyes narrowed farther before understanding came over his gaze. He lifted his chin and looked at me, his jaw tight. "I'm flattered you're jealous."

"Jealous?" I hissed. "I'm not jealous. I'm just pissed."

"Same thing." The corner of his mouth rose in a smile.

I shook my head and held the towel over my body. "You're

an asshole. Get out of my room." I stormed into the living room. That way I could shut the door.

He was close behind me, making sure I couldn't shut him out of anywhere. "As much as I'm enjoying this, it's not how it seems."

"If you think I'm stupid—"

He grabbed me by the elbow and jerked me toward him. He pulled the towel away and tossed it off to the side so I couldn't grab it again. "My models kiss me all the time. You've seen them do it. Doesn't mean I fucked them."

I wanted to believe him, but I felt stupid for believing that. I twisted out of his grasp.

He held me tighter, dragging me against his body. "Muse, if I fucked someone, I wouldn't hide it from you. I don't give a damn if I hurt your feelings or not. I'm free to do whatever I want. You're the one who has to keep her legs closed to anyone but me. That's the deal—that's why I bought you."

It only partially consoled me. "You're an asshole."

"How else did you think this was going to be?" he demanded. "That we would be exclusive forever?"

It was a stupid thing to think. I never should have assumed it in the first place. He called me his muse and bought me for so much money that I thought I meant more to him. I thought I would be enough for him. "If you're fucking me all the time, why do you need anyone else?"

His eyes shifted back and forth slightly as he stared at me, his fingertips digging into my skin. The gaze was intense and long. It didn't seem like he was going to say anything at all. It wasn't surprising that he was an incredible designer since he could stare at something without blinking for such a long period of time. "I haven't been with another woman since the day I met you. But don't get confused about the nature of our relationship. You're my toy. I'm the only man who can enjoy you because I own you. But I will enjoy other women when I feel like it. I'm not committed to you whatsoever."

I already knew he would say that, but it didn't minimize the sting. I tried to yank my elbow out of his hold, but his grip was too tight. "I'm not letting you give me anything."

"I always wear a condom."

"You didn't wear a condom with me."

"Different. You're the only woman I would do that with."

I tried to twist again. "Is that supposed to make me feel special?"

"I'm just telling you that you have nothing to worry about."

"Then we're wearing condoms too."

He chuckled like I'd made a joke. "You don't call the shots here, Muse. I do."

"That's bullshit, and we both know it. If I want something, I get it. You act like you're this asshole, but you give me more freedom than you realize." I yanked my arm down and finally got free. I grabbed the towel from the floor and covered myself with it.

"That's where you're wrong, Muse." He slowly approached me, his arms by his sides and his jaw clenched with barely restrained anger. He adopted an unthreatening stance, but he'd never seemed so terrifying. "I made things easy on you for the first time." His hand moved to my elbow, and he grabbed it gently before he turned me around. I cooperated, feeling his quiet hostility. He grabbed the back of my neck and then shoved me into the couch.

I fell, losing my grip on my towel.

His pants dropped to the floor, and he pinned me down, my ass up and my face pressed to the cushion. The towel slipped to the floor, and now I was naked, my hair still damp. He got behind me quickly, and before I could fight back, he shoved his hard cock inside me in one swift thrust.

I lurched forward, gripping the couch cushions for balance.

He kept my face pinned down and leaned over me, his big cock buried inside my tightness. I barely had time to adjust to him, and he was burrowing through like he owned me. He squeezed my neck harder. "But I won't be easy on you again. You're just a trophy, a product in exchange for money. Don't forget that you're nothing—and you'll always be nothing."

I WASN'T sure what I expected from Conway. Sometimes he seemed like a nice guy. At other times, he seemed like a sadist. He gave me the gentleness and respect I craved, but then he took it away with the snap of a finger.

Then I was reduced to nothing.

He spent so much money purchasing me that I assumed I would be his only mistress. I was the inspiration for his lingerie, so why would he want to fuck someone else? He said I was his fantasy, so how could some other woman take my place? It wasn't jealousy that I felt. It simply didn't add up.

He fucked me harder than he ever had on the couch, making me bleed a little. When he was finished, he pulled on his pants and walked out without saying a word to me. He finished his business, and then our conversation was dismissed.

I stayed in my room for the rest of the day, not wanting to see him after our argument. I didn't want to see his face, and I certainly didn't want him to see mine. He fucked me like a whore, pressing my face into the cushion with my ass in the air. But then something terrible happened.

He made me come.

I hid it as best I could, but I suspected he knew.

Conway always knew.

Now I was ashamed, embarrassed that I enjoyed a man who treated me like an object instead of a human.

What was wrong with me?

Dante knocked on my bedroom door. "Dinner is served, miss."

I stared at the solid wood door from my seat on the bed. I'd been locked inside my bedroom all evening, spending my time watching TV or reading. The last thing I wanted to do was sit across from Conway like everything was fine. "I'm not hungry."

Dante's footsteps didn't sound against the floor. He stayed in the exact same spot. "Conway is expecting you."

"I don't give a damn what he expects, Dante." I ran my fingers through my hair, hoping Conway wouldn't burst through the door the second Dante told him the news. It forced my heart rate to spike in fear, even though I shouldn't be afraid of that man.

Dante's sigh was audible through the door. "Alright, miss." His footsteps faded away.

I waited ten minutes for Conway's presence to fill the hallway and leak through the crack in the doorway, but it never came. When thirty minutes came and went, I knew he wasn't coming.

My stomach growled, but I ignored it.

I spent the next few hours watching TV and reading before I went to bed. I washed my face, threw my hair in a bun, and then pulled the covers back on my perfectly made bed so I could slip beneath the sheets.

That's when I heard his footsteps.

Just like in *Jurassic Park* when the dinosaur's heavy footfalls could be seen in the vibration of the water, an ominous feeling spread over me. My pulse quickened in my neck, and I stared at the door as I waited. I didn't have a lock on my door, which I was certain was intentional. There was nothing that could stop him from getting to me.

In a fluid motion, he opened the door and stepped inside. He was only in his sweatpants, his torso a wall of muscle, valleys, and tanned skin. All of his muscles shifted and moved together as he walked. He didn't need a crown on his head or a ten-thousand-dollar suit on his body to look powerful. Even when he was reduced to nothing but skin, he was more powerful than any man in the world.

Eyes trained on me, he approached my bed and then pulled down his sweats and boxers at the same time. His enormous cock popped out, nine inches of length and more than a few inches of girth. The first few times we'd had sex, it hurt. That probably wasn't normal, but I think his large size was responsible for my prolonged discomfort.

I didn't resist because there was no point. It didn't matter how pissed I was, he would get what he wanted. He'd dominated me just a few hours ago, putting himself in charge and reminding me just how insignificant I was.

He threw back the covers over my legs and then dragged me to the edge of the bed until my ass hung over the mattress. I was in a long nightdress, so he pulled off my panties and hiked the dress over my tits. Then he directed his fat crown against my entrance and pushed inside.

I tensed at the intrusion, my body resisting the initial push. He stretched me wide apart, pushing my body to new limits. He made me feel fuller than I'd ever felt, his cock pushing on all my walls and making me squeeze around him.

He stood at the bedside like a statue of a powerful solider. He grabbed my hips and pulled me closer to him, getting me perfectly situated so he could thrust and enjoy me.

I breathed through the stretch, felt my body trying to acclimate to his enormity.

He paused as he stared down at me, his cold gaze commanding me with just the strength of his look. He reached his hand out and wrapped his fingers around my neck, making it abundantly clear I was his to enjoy. He didn't squeeze me, just tightened his grasp enough to feel my pulse. The veins on his hands and forearms popped with his maneuvers, the chiseled lines of his muscle noticeable even in the darkness.

Then he thrust, moving inside me at a steady pace. He rocked the bed with his movements, making it shake as he moved his dick through my tightness. At first, it was rough. But I felt my body loosen as I rocked with him, felt my wetness emerge and sheathe him.

I looked at the ceiling, embarrassed that my body would betray me so coldly.

We fucked in silence, our breathing filling the quiet room. His hands reached up and grabbed my tits, palming them with his rough skin. He squeezed me hard, making my nipples ache as he flicked them harshly.

But I felt myself moan in response.

God, why?

He hooked his arms behind my knees and pinned my legs against my sides. He moved his weight to his arms, leaning over me slightly and deepening the angle of his thrusts. His eyes were on me now, watching me shake with the momentum he gave to our bodies.

He didn't kiss me.

My fingers locked around his wrists so I had something to hold on to. The tightness inside my pussy didn't feel as painful as it used to. Now my body had stretched in response to his size. Now I felt the pleasure and none of the pain.

He finally wore me out.

My eyes shifted to the mirror on my dresser, which reflected the sight of his tight ass. He clenched every time he thrust, the hunk of muscle leading to a sculpted back. It was powerful and beautiful, sexy to stare at.

I needed to stop staring at his ass. If I didn't, I would come.

"Eyes on me." His deep voice interrupted our heavy

breathing in the darkness. The baritone immediately commanded me.

My eyes returned to his face. The concentration of his gaze was just as sexy as his ass. His hard jaw immediately tightened, and when his eyes burned with intensity, I knew he was enjoying me. His lips were parted as he breathed, and the sweat began to collect on his forehead. Shit, I was going to come.

"Don't fight me. Enjoy me."

My nails dug into his forearms as I felt his dick hit me in the perfect spot. "No."

He increased his thrusts, hitting me harder and harder.

Now I didn't stand a chance. This sexy man held my body hostage. He could control it like a puppet. He could even control my mind. I was powerless to stop it, unable to combat my natural arousal. The first time I saw him on TV, I thought he was the most handsome man in the world. And now he was fucking me so good that I couldn't resist.

He closed his eyes for a moment and moaned. "Muse, you're so wet…"

I'd never felt so pathetic in my life—and aroused.

"Come."

"No…" I fought him as hard as I could, trying not to think about the pleasure he was causing between my legs.

He fucked me harder, grinding against me. "Now."

My mind resisted him, but my body couldn't. I came with a moan, my head rolling back and my nails cutting into his forearms. His name erupted from my throat naturally, and I realized how much of a prisoner I truly was. "Yes…"

His hand grabbed my neck again, and he thrust into me hard, hitting me deep between my legs. He gave a guttural moan before he released, his dick throbbing inside me. He dumped his seed, its weight and warmth immediately noticeable within me. He gave a final moan once he was finished. His dick slowly started to soften, and his fingers stopped gripping me so tightly. Sweat had formed on his chest, and now he looked even sexier than before.

He slowly pulled out of me, some of his come spilling onto the floor. He left me there as he grabbed his boxers and pants and pulled them up. Then he left my bedroom without turning around. He didn't kiss me goodnight or extend any affection. We hadn't slept in the same bed since the first time we were together.

Like I really meant nothing to him, he just walked out.

And didn't look back.

2

Conway

Muse was finally understanding our arrangement.

She was mine to do with whatever I wished. She had no rights. She wasn't entitled to an opinion. Her only purpose was to take my cock and enjoy it. I paid a fortune for her, and that debt reduced her to a beautiful woman I got to use on a daily basis.

She needed to accept it.

I was free to fuck whomever I wanted. I could have any woman I felt like having, whether it was at work or on the town. She had no right to expect anything from me. For me to be faithful would require me to care about her.

I didn't give a damn about her.

The sooner she understood that, the easier her life would be.

I was only kind to her once—and that was because I didn't have the balls to be anything less than gentle. I was a selfish asshole who only cared about money and fame, but I didn't want to brutally take away something she'd held on to for so long.

I couldn't do that.

But she shouldn't confuse my niceness for weakness.

I was still a dick.

Now that our relationship had been straightened out, the fucking was what I wanted it to be. When I wanted pussy, I barged into her room and took it. She could lie there and fight the pleasure all she wanted.

We both knew she would come every time.

When I woke up the following morning, I had my morning swim and then sat at the table where Dante served breakfast. But he only had a place setting for one.

She was still fighting me. "Tell Sapphire to join us."

"I already tried, sir. Says she's not hungry."

She was going to starve herself just to be defiant? "Bring her a tray and tell her to be ready for me in fifteen minutes." She would know exactly what be ready meant.

"Yes, sir." Dante walked away and left me alone to enjoy my meal.

I could force her to skip breakfast, but I didn't get off on the idea of her starving. It wasn't a battle I would take pride in winning, so I just let her get her way. She could refuse to have meals with me, but polite conversation wasn't that important to me anyway.

I would fuck her once I was finished.

I read the newspaper and looked through my emails. Most of them were from Nicole. Her emails flooded my inbox at every hour of the day, from five in the afternoon until two in the morning. She never seemed to stop working, but she was paid the big bucks for that reason. She probably didn't have much of a personal life.

My phone rang on the table, and I looked at the screen to see a name I couldn't ignore. Breakfast was a quiet time for me, when I would read the newspaper and enjoy my coffee. But whenever my mom called, nothing else seemed to matter.

I took the call. "Hey, Mom. How are you?"

She had a voice that was naturally elegant. I could picture her deep brown hair and blue eyes just by listening to the sound of her voice. She'd always been a lot more easygoing than my father, which was interesting because in most other areas, it was the opposite. My mother knew how to smile, knew how to enjoy life. My father was serious nearly all the time. "Hey, Con. I hope I'm not interrupting anything."

Even if she were, I would never tell her. "Just having breakfast on the terrace. It's a beautiful day."

"It is. Your father and I just had breakfast with Vanessa in Milan. We were in the area and thought the three of us would stop by." My parents lived five hours away in the southern part of Italy. They preferred wine country, where the summers were truly hot and humid.

"Are you here on business?"

"Your father had a meeting with a restaurant owner in Milan."

"That's nice." My father was almost sixty, but he'd never slowed down. When I was growing up, he never took sick days and always went to work. He loved to spend time with my mother, but he always needed his own space. Now he was still working even though he could have retired decades ago. That was how he was wired—and I was exactly the same way.

"We were thinking of stopping by for lunch. You're at your home in Verona, right?"

My thoughts immediately went to the woman living on my property. I couldn't hide her forever, but I wasn't ready to reveal her either. "I'll come to you, Mom. I'm sure you guys have already been driving a lot lately."

"We don't mind. Your father wants to see Carbine."

Oh, fuck. I couldn't deny my mother a second time. "What time were you thinking?"

"Noon?" she asked. "Unless you're working today?"

It was Saturday. I didn't usually go to Milan on the weekends. My other studio was here, and Nicole was always available through email. Now that I'd brought Sapphire with me, I didn't have a lot of incentive to drive to Milan anymore—not when my inspiration lived with me. "No, I'm off."

"Alright. I'm so excited to see you, Con. I miss you so much…" The maternal side of her emerged, her voice reaching a new tone as the sincerity came through the phone. I was almost thirty, but my mother still loved me like I was five.

"I miss you too, Mama."

WHEN I FOUND the empty breakfast tray in Muse's room, I knew she'd already left for the stables.

I was hoping she would still be there so I could have a morning fuck.

I walked down the dirt path and reached the barn and stables. Muse was there, carrying a bridle and reins to the tack room. She hung it on the metal hook then wiped her hands on her denim jeans. Even when she was dressed like a cowgirl, she still looked sexy. Made me wonder if I could make a design to complement it, maybe have a photographer shoot her right here in the barn. "Muse."

She turned my way, her hair in a braid over one shoulder. Her eyes narrowed in a hostile smolder.

Fuck, she was hot. I loved that pissed look she gave me. All

I had to do was fuck her to make it go away. I'd claimed her innocence and changed her into a sexual woman. I made her enjoy sex, made her enjoy me.

I walked toward her then gave Marco a meaningful look.

He disappeared.

"I have a lot of work to do, so what is it?" she asked, taking a step back and keeping distance between us.

"I need you to head back to the house and stay in your bedroom for the rest of the day."

"Why?"

I glared at her.

"It's not even ten yet," she said. "I have a lot of work to do and plenty of time to get it done."

"That's what I pay Marco for. So get in the house."

"Why?" she repeated.

"Because I said so," I hissed.

We were out in the open with a witness just around the corner. She probably thought she was safe out there, that there was nothing I could do to get her to cooperate.

She shouldn't underestimate me.

She turned away. "I like being out here."

I grabbed her by the elbow and jerked her back toward me. "And you can be out here tomorrow. But for today, you need to go inside. Don't make me ask you again. I'll take you in one of those stalls and fuck you with your jeans around your ankles. Try me, Muse. Try me."

She didn't jerk away from my grip, but the menace in her eyes suggested she was considering it. "Tell me why."

"Doesn't matter."

"It does to me."

My hand tightened on her elbow, and I pulled her closer to me. "I have company coming."

"And you don't want them to see me." Her eyes narrowed in disgust. "Of course…I'm your dirty little secret."

"Or maybe I just don't want to share you."

"Who is it?"

"My family."

Her hostility slowly faded away. "Your family?"

"My parents and sister. They're coming over for lunch, and they don't need to see you."

She pulled her arm away slowly. "You're going to hide me from them forever?"

"Not sure yet."

"They won't even notice me over here. Tell them I'm just a member of your staff."

Now my patience was really waning. I'd never had to

argue with someone so much. My orders were followed without question, and her constant inquisition was really pissing me off. "If you don't get your ass in the house, I'll slap that pretty face of yours until my handprint is marked on your cheek. Do you understand me?"

Instead of taking off in fright, she stood her ground. Then she did something I never could have anticipated. She stepped closer to me, getting right in my face. "Do it. Slap me." She placed her hands on her hips and squared her shoulders. She even turned her face so I had perfect access to her cheek.

I'd slapped my sister when I was seven years old, and my father beat my ass for it. He told me to never hit a woman as long as I lived. If I did, he would hunt me down and beat my ass again—no matter how old I was. I wasn't afraid of the pain, but I was certainly afraid of his disappointment.

The tense silence stretched between us. Muse stared at me with the same hostility as before, hardly blinking as she met my gaze. Then she finally turned away and headed to the house. "That's what I thought, Conway." She walked away, her hips shaking as she made her exit.

I watched her, infuriated, hating myself for letting her prove me wrong. I should have given her the beating of a lifetime to put her in her place. But my anger was mixed with the deepest wave of arousal I'd ever felt. Something about her telling me off got my heart racing. She didn't hesitate before she called me an asshole, and she didn't hesitate before she called my bluff.

Fucking hot.

———

I WALKED into her bedroom and found her pile of dirty clothes and boots in the hamper with the plastic lining. She stood at the dresser, looking through her underwear drawer in search of something to wear. She was buck naked, her braid still hanging down one shoulder.

I stared at her perky ass, the lines under her cheeks perfect. I was hard before I stepped into the room, but now I was even harder than a rock. I crossed the room and wrapped both of my arms around her waist. Then I tossed her on the bed, her back hitting the bed that the maids made shortly after she woke up.

She didn't fight me, but she still wore the same look of loathing.

I dropped my bottoms and didn't bother with my shirt. I climbed on top of her and pinned her down with my size. My cock was inside her instantly, and I fucked her hard. There was no beginning, middle, or end. It was a just a hard fuck, my cock stretching her small pussy before I even gave her a chance to get used to me.

Almost instantly, that hostile look faded away. Color filled her cheeks, and her eyes became lidded and heavy. Like a patient failing to fight off anesthesia, she couldn't resist the spell her hormones were casting over her.

All I knew was I needed to fuck her—and I needed to do

it hard and fast. A million sensations rushed through me in that moment. I was pissed and horny at the same time. I deepened the angle and folded her underneath me, using her for my own perverseness.

She started to moan because she wasn't bothering to fight it this time.

Good.

I liked the way she stood up to me, called my bluff when she didn't know what would happen. It was dangerous and stupid, and I respected her bravery. I respected her for speaking her mind and holding her ground. Anyone else I interacted with would have flinched at my intimidation, but she never did.

"Slap me."

She held on to my wrists, the place where she usually touched me. Her hands never explored my body unless I was kissing her. She touched as little of me as possible as part of her resistance.

"Slap me," I repeated.

Uncertainty was in her eyes.

It wasn't a trick, a way to give me the opportunity to slap her back. I really just wanted her to hit me.

She finally hit her palm against my face, but it was weak.

"Harder."

She hit me again.

"Come on, Muse. Show me how much you hate me."

This time, she put all of her strength into the hit. She put her whole arm behind it, hitting me with enough force to make my entire face tingle.

It was exactly what I wanted.

I pictured doing the same to her, making her feel the pain I just felt.

And that was enough for me.

I came inside her, filling her perfect pussy with come.

The disappointment in her eyes was unmistakable. She didn't find her release because I didn't give her a chance.

It was intentional.

"That's for your little stunt back there." I pulled out of her, letting my come drip onto her bedding. "And if you touch yourself, I'll punish you even more." I didn't wipe myself off before I pulled my bottoms back on. I had to get ready before my family came over, and I didn't want to stay and chat with her, not when I was still pissed at her. "Stay here until I tell you otherwise."

"I'm not a dog, Conway." She closed her legs and sat upright, looking thoroughly fucked and beautiful.

"No, you aren't. But you're my prisoner all the same."

———

THE BLACK SUV came into the roundabout, black-tinted

windows with bulletproof glass. The passenger door opened, and my mother stepped out in a long white dress with tan strappy sandals. Her brown hair was in curls down her chest, and the sunglasses on her face couldn't hide the happiness in her eyes.

She gave me the same smile I'd received my entire childhood.

She hopped slightly as she made her way to me, the excitement written all over her face. I was a grown man and had been out of the house since the day I turned eighteen, but to her, I was still crawling across the floor in a diaper.

A foot shorter than me, she wrapped her arms around my waist and squeezed me with the strength of a professional wrestler. "My son…" Her cheek rested against my chest, and she breathed a happy sigh.

I squeezed her back, her petiteness similar to Muse's. "Hey, Mom."

"You're bigger every time I see you."

"I hope not."

She chuckled. "You know what I mean." She pulled away then placed her hand on my cheek. She looked into my expression like I was a painting rather than a person. "You look so much like your father. It makes me very happy."

"I've always been a little disappointed about it."

She chuckled again then pulled her hand away.

Vanessa came next, her brown hair pulled into an updo and her olive skin beautiful under the summer sun. She wore a strapless yellow dress that was tight around her slender waist. She pulled her sunglasses off her face as she walked toward me. Her eyes were mixed with annoyance but also excitement. She was pissed about the stunt I'd pulled a few weeks ago, but she'd get over it. "Brother." She hugged me.

"Sister." I blew off her hug by giving her a quick pat on the back instead.

She stuck her tongue out at me. "You're lucky I have to love you no matter what."

"You're even more lucky."

She rolled her eyes and walked into the house.

My father came next, in black jeans and a black t-shirt. I hardly saw him wear anything else except that color. In fact, I'd never seen him wear the color white. He walked up the steps toward me, his moss green eyes locked on to my face with intense concentration. It was difficult to tell if he was angry or not because he seemed angry all the time—at least he looked that way.

Mom stood off to the side, watching us as my father moved closer.

He approached me in the entryway, his face clearer now that the bright sun wasn't washing out his features. His jaw was a hard line, despite his age. His face was slightly weathered from sun exposure, but it made his skin tight and gave him a glow of youth. His shoulders were still strong, and his forearms were corded with veins. My dad had been ripped his entire life, and even without seeing him with his shirt off, it was obvious that he was still in great shape. Ever since I could remember, my father ran around the estate every morning and then used his private gym afterward. There were times when I'd look out the window in the morning on summer vacation and see his outline on the other side of the vineyards. He'd always been a role model to me, the definition of what a strong man should be. The strong and silent type, he didn't say anything unless it was worth being said. He showed my mother he loved her by the way he looked at her, the way he touched her. He commanded the respect of his children through his silence, not his anger. He laid the foundation of exactly what I should be, and because of him, I'd become the man I was today. "Son."

"Father, how are you?"

He never answered me. All he did was stare at my face, studying my expression like he'd never seen me before. We went months without seeing each other sometimes since we lived so far away from one another. So when he did see me, it was always with this same kind of inspection. "Better now." My father greeted his clients and friends with just looks. His brother was his best friend, and I'd never seen them hug in my life. My father hardly extended a handshake, even to his clients. But he'd always been different with us. It was the only time he showed affection. He wrapped his arms around me and hugged me.

I hugged him back. It didn't matter how old I was. I would always live for the approval of my father. His pride meant a lot to me. He was the biggest role model I'd ever had. He expected a lot of me.

He held me for a long time, like he always did. Even if there were people around, he did the same thing. Then he pulled away, cupped the back of my head, and planted a kiss on my forehead.

Mom's smile widened.

He patted me on the arm and turned away. "Beautiful day, isn't it?"

I watched his strong shoulders shift as he walked. He was over six feet tall, and the day I'd reached his height, I knew it made him choke up a bit. "Yeah, it is." I watched him grab my mother's hand and walk inside after Vanessa.

I joined them a second later.

FATHER and I walked to the fence where Carbine grazed. He had his own plot of land, separate from the mares because he was territorial and aggressive. Marco had extensive experience, but even he struggled to control the stallion. I told him Muse wasn't allowed to go anywhere near Carbine because it was way too dangerous.

Dad stopped at the fence and clicked his tongue.

Carbine raised his head from the grass, his ears twitching.

He turned his head our way, his mane flowing in the slight breeze. His large brown eyes settled on us, and he gave a quiet neigh before he trotted to us.

Dad smiled as he eyed the horse. "Beautiful steed." He held out the carrot.

Carbine stuffed it down in a few bites.

Dad scratched him behind the ear. "He's looking good."

"Very." I ran my hand up his snout, feeling the short hair that shifted under my fingertips. His warm breaths fell over me, and the sound of horse flies accompanied him. His dark hair was shiny under the hot sun, and his beautiful black form contrasted against the white fence and the green grass.

"Marco does a good job?"

"Yes." But Muse had been doing a great job as well. Marco told me she busted her ass around the stables, shoveling shit and restocking hay like she was born a country girl. She wasn't afraid to get her hands dirty or put in a hard day of labor. Marco loved having her around, and it made his job a million times easier—and more enjoyable.

It made me more fascinated with her. She was a strong woman with a lot of potential. It really was a shame she'd gotten mixed up with such bullshit. Her brother was dead, but I wanted to kill him anyway.

He deserved to die twice.

We stared at the horse for a few more minutes before we walked up the path back to the house.

"Do you ride often?" He walked beside me with a perfectly straight back, carrying himself like a man in his twenties rather than his sixties.

"Haven't had time."

"I know how that is."

"How's the wine business?"

"Good," he answered. "Business is good."

"And Uncle Cane?"

"A dumbass, like always."

I chuckled because I knew he didn't mean that. "Aunt Adelina?"

"She's good too. She's not a dumbass."

"Lucky for him."

We'd left Mom and Vanessa on the patio, where they drank sangria and lay by the pool as they waited for Dante to prepare lunch.

"So you're in town for business?" I asked.

"There's a restaurant owner up here that wants to start hosting weddings. So we talked about a deal where he could have a collection of wines by the barrel. He makes a commission, and I make a commission."

"Sounds like a good deal."

"How's the fashion business? Your mom and I watched the show a few weeks ago. It was great."

My dad never seemed awkward about my livelihood. He must have known what my lifestyle was like, but he never asked me about it. I was almost thirty and unmarried, but neither of my parents asked about my desire to start my own family. I knew my parents had been my age when they got together. Before that, it didn't seem like either of them had had any significant relationships.

When we reached the terrace, my heart stopped in my chest.

My mother and sister were sitting together at the table with their glasses of red sangria. But a third person had joined them.

Muse.

She fucking disobeyed me.

In a long blue dress with her hair in curls, she looked like a supermodel ready for a fashion shoot. She wore tan strappy sandals and a large sunhat to keep the sun off her shoulders. With her legs crossed and perfect grace, she looked like the model who was the headliner of my show.

When she heard us approach, she turned to look at me.

With a big fucking smile on her face.

Oh, this was intentional.

If my family wasn't there right that moment, I might actually have slapped her.

And slapped her fucking hard.

"Hey, *honey*." Muse rose to greet me, her drink still in her hand. She walked up to me, carrying all the confidence in the world. She had me by the balls, and she knew it. She tilted her head up to kiss me, her eyes full of glee.

It was the only time when I truly didn't want to kiss her. I didn't want to feel those arrogant lips against mine. I wanted to grab her by the hair and yank her into my bedroom. Just when I thought I'd claimed the upper hand in this arrangement, she fucked me over. "Hey, *baby*." I craned my neck down and gave her the coldest kiss I'd ever given anyone. I even kissed my mother on the cheek better than that.

She turned to my father and extended her hand. "So nice to meet you, Mr. Barsetti. Your son talks about you often. I'm Sapphire."

My dad eyed me before he took her hand, and unfortunately, a small smile spread across his lips.

Shit.

He shook her hand and turned his gaze back to her. "It's lovely to meet you as well." He leaned in and kissed her on the cheek.

Fuck, my dad never kissed a woman on the cheek except my sister.

"Can I get you something to drink?" Sapphire asked. "Your son tells me you like scotch. I'm a scotch drinker too."

This couldn't be happening.

My dad smiled again. "I'd love some, sweetheart."

No. No. No.

"Coming right up." Muse walked to the bar to prepare the drinks.

My father turned back to me once she was out of earshot. "She seems like a lovely woman."

I could tell my dad already liked her—and he didn't like anyone.

Mom joined our conversation, grinning wider than I'd ever seen her. "Why didn't you tell us about your girlfriend?"

Muse had caught me off guard, and I didn't know what to say. I couldn't tell my parents the truth, so I had to lie. I was at her mercy because she'd outsmarted me. "I wanted it to be a surprise, I guess."

Mom turned to my father. "They live together."

My father's expression hardened slightly. "So she's more than just your girlfriend."

Fuck.

Vanessa joined our huddle. "Con, I really like her. I always thought you'd be into dumb bimbos, but I guess I was wrong. She's awesome."

"I like her too," Mom said. "She's sweet."

I kept my features steady, but a storm was brewing deep inside me. Muse had crossed a line with this. She was making my family believe in a lie—and I didn't lie to my family. She was messing with their hopes and feelings.

I could strangle her.

Muse returned with two glasses of scotch. She handed one to my father and one to me.

She didn't even ask what I wanted. She just knew. And she just proved to my family that she knew me too.

I definitely had underestimated this woman.

———

VANESSA SAT BESIDE MUSE, immediately taking a liking to her. "So, when did this start?"

I sat across from Muse, and I eyed her coldly in response. If she wanted to continue with this lie, she'd be the one making it up.

"About six months." She held her glass of sangria and took a drink before she set it down. "And then he asked me to move in with him three weeks ago."

That last part was partially true, but I never asked her to move in with me—I told her to.

"Aww," Vanessa said. "I didn't think my brother had a romantic bone in his body."

She was right. I didn't.

Mom turned to me, accusation in her eyes. "I'm surprised my son didn't tell me he's been seeing someone for six months…" Disappointment was in her eyes, lots of it.

I glared at Muse harder.

"Since we work together, he wanted to keep it a secret for a while." Muse continued to lie effortlessly, doing so well, I almost believed her too. "I did a few photo shoots with him, and we didn't want the other models to feel like he was giving me priority because of our romantic relationship."

"That's why you look so familiar," Vanessa said. "You were the headliner of his last show."

"Yes," Muse said. "I was. Conway is a brilliant designer. I'm honored I get to wear his clothes."

She had a funny way of showing it.

My dad didn't say anything. He listened to the conversation and ate the meal Dante prepared for him.

"What brought you to Italy?" my mother asked.

I couldn't picture myself going along with this fable for the next decade. I would have to keep these lies in check anytime I was around my family. And then I couldn't be seen with other women because it would seem like I was a cheater…and my family would be extremely disappointed in me if they saw that. The idea of being with another woman hadn't even crossed my mind since I met Muse, but that wasn't the point. She was the prisoner, and I was the master. How could I let her flip it on me? Now, I was at her mercy. I could never let my family know what really happened between Muse and me. My mother would never forgive me if she knew Muse was just a prisoner in my mansion. And the disappointment from my father would kill me.

"I'd always wanted to be a model for Barsetti Lingerie, so I left New York in pursuit of my dream. I met Conway, and he took a chance on me." Muse wove this story so well. It was a bunch of bullshit, but she managed not to incriminate herself. Both of my parents saw through bullshit pretty easily, but neither one of them seemed to catch on to this. It was probably because they assumed if I ever owned up to a relationship with someone, she must be the one…since I never had relationships.

She had me under her thumb.

"Will you continue to be in the shows?" Mom asked.

I refused to participate in this conversation, so I didn't say anything.

"Conway is a little bit jealous when it comes to me, so he took me out of his lineup." She stared at me across the table, a knowing smile on her lips.

"Aww…" My mom's eyes softened. "Just like his father."

Fuck, this was bad.

If I didn't change the subject, it would just continue. My mom and sister were already infatuated with the woman they thought I was in love with, and the longer I let it go on, the worse it would get. "Vanessa, how's the painting going?"

"Great," Vanessa said. "We started doing watercolors this week, and I love it. I didn't think I would love anything more than traditional oil painting, but all the colors and the drips really fascinate me."

"Have you made anything?" It was the first time my father spoke.

"I just finished my first painting this week," Vanessa answered.

"I'd love to see it." My father went out of his way to be invested in everything we did. He obviously didn't care about art whatsoever, but he made it clear he cared about whatever his daughter cared about.

"I'll show it to you," Vanessa said. She turned back to Muse. "Do you know about the stunt my brother pulled a few weeks ago?"

I narrowed my eyes. "Shut it, Vanessa."

Muse grinned. "You have to tell me now."

"Alright." Vanessa set her napkin down. "So I went on a date with this nice guy I go to school with…"

My dad suddenly stopped eating, setting down his fork and reaching for his scotch right away. There hadn't been a single boy who ever came to the house as long as Vanessa lived there. Not even for school dances. When it came to my sister dating, my father turned into a different person.

"And Conway watched us have dinner from across the street, followed us as he walked me home, and stood in the shadows as we said goodnight on the doorstep. Then he followed the guy for a few blocks." Vanessa rolled her eyes. "That's the kind of man you live with, just in case you didn't know…"

When Muse turned to look at me, she didn't regard me with the same coldness my sister did. It was the softest expression she'd ever given me. She actually seemed touched by what my sister said.

Yes, I wasn't an asshole all the time.

"He's such a psychopath," Vanessa said. "A complete breach of privacy."

"I don't give a damn." I drank my scotch to kill the nerves. "There are a lot of assholes out there, Vanessa. You don't know that because I've made sure you've never met one. There are—"

"Enough." My father's voice was quiet, but it was filled with so much anger. He finished his scotch and set the empty glass on the table.

Even Vanessa shut her mouth.

Muse eyed my father but didn't say another word.

I knew exactly why my father ended the conversation. He'd

told me what happened to his sister, Vanessa's namesake. It never stopped haunting him, even now. He protected my sister every second of the day before she moved out, and he didn't even realize it. As the man's oldest son, it was my responsibility to take care of our family if something happened to him, so he dropped the burden on my shoulders.

And I took that responsibility seriously.

MY FAMILY finally left when the sun set.

Thank fucking god.

My mother kissed me on the cheek. "I love you."

"I love you too, Mom."

She squeezed me hard around the waist. "I really like Sapphire. She's lovely."

I forced a smile. "I'm glad. She's very sweet."

"I knew it was only a matter of time before you found the right woman." She kissed me on the cheek again before she walked to the car with Vanessa.

My father kissed Sapphire on the cheek. "It was very nice meeting you. I look forward to seeing you more often."

"You too," she said. "Conway has a very nice family."

"My son treats you well?"

Why did my father have to ask that?

Sapphire's smile didn't falter, but her eyes definitely did. "Yes. Your son is a good man."

"I'm glad to hear that." He turned to me next, his eyes examining me like two X-rays. "You should bring Sapphire down to Tuscany. Give her a tour of your childhood home and the winery."

"I'm sure I will."

He hugged me. "Love you, son."

I hugged him back. "Love you too, Father."

He cupped the back of my head and kissed me on the forehead before he walked away. They piled into the car and rolled down their windows so they could wave as they drove off.

Sapphire came to my side and wrapped her arm around my waist as she waved at my family.

The second their car was out of sight, I dropped my hand and turned my hostile stare on her.

Her smile was long gone, and her arm was no longer around my waist. She placed her hands on her hips and stared at me with the same menace.

"You have no idea what you're doing."

"I think I do," she said confidently. "Things are going to be different around here. Cross me, and I'll tell your family who you really are."

"You're crossing a line."

"Like you haven't crossed the line a million times over."

I'd done a lot of things I wasn't proud of, but I'd never cared about my image before. People could think whatever they wanted about me. But my family was a different story. Their approval meant a lot to me. I couldn't stand my parents' disappointment. If my father knew I was keeping Muse against her will, he'd beat me to the brink of death. "What do you want?"

"New rules."

I couldn't believe I was negotiating with a woman I bought for a hundred million dollars. "What the fuck does that mean?"

"I want to be an equal in this house."

My name was on the deed to the property, so she would never be equal.

"No bossing me around. I do what I want, and I have every right to refuse you."

Why didn't I just tell my parents I was out of town? I never should have let them come over here unless Muse was locked away behind soundproof walls. "Be careful, Muse."

"Be careful?" she asked. "You're the one who should be careful."

"If you want free will, then just walk out," I threatened. "Leave. I'll tell everyone that I've let you go. I'm sure Knuckles will find that information most useful." Perhaps

I needed to remind her what I saved her from. She had me by the nuts, but I had her by the tits.

Her anger died away slightly. "You're right. I don't want to leave because I have nowhere to go. Outside these four walls and your protection, I'm absolutely nothing. I get it." Her voice broke, and she swallowed. "But I want to be treated differently in here. I want rights and respect."

If I didn't respect her, she wouldn't have any rights at all.

"First of all, you knock on my door. I decide whether I want to let you in or not."

I didn't like that one bit.

"I decide if we have sex or not."

I actually growled. "You forget how much I paid to save your life."

"And you forget I'm a human being and shouldn't have been sold like cattle in the first place."

"Not my problem," I snapped. "You got yourself into that situation in the first place."

"Whatever." She held up her hand. "Thirdly, I do what I want when I want. If I want to work in the stables all day, I will. If I don't want to eat with you, I won't."

"So you're basically just some woman that I completely support and from whom I get nothing in return?" I asked incredulously. "Because if you're completely useless to me, then I may as well just kick you out."

"No, I won't be useless to you. But you're going to treat me like a human being from now on. Consider it a compromise. I work so I have a place to live. You treat me with respect so you keep your glowing reputation to your parents. That's fair if you ask me."

If I weren't so close with my family, I would just tell them the truth so we could return to the previous arrangement. I liked doing what I wanted, bossing her around whenever I felt like it. It was one of the best perks of the entire situation. "You're missing something."

"What?" She crossed her arms over her chest.

"My parents actually believe this bullshit relationship is real."

"So?"

"So?" I snapped. "Now I have to keep up the charade. You think I want to do that?"

"You will if you want to keep your end of the deal."

My palm twitched because I wanted to slap that beautiful face. "We're messing with their feelings."

"People have relationships all the time. People break up all the time."

"But my parents think this is serious. I've never introduced them to a woman before, so they probably think I'm going to marry you or something stupid like that."

"Not my problem," she said coldly.

I never should have underestimated this woman. She managed to escape from Knuckles in the first place and get hired as one of my models. She was able to win me over, to convince me to buy her for a hundred million dollars. She was no average person.

Looked like I'd met my match.

3

Sapphire

I sat on my bed with an open book. My day had been spent in the stables, and my shoulders were sore in a way they'd never been before. I'd never truly had a hard day's work in New York—not like I did here. My fingers started to callus and my muscles toned, but I enjoyed it.

But I still hadn't ridden yet.

Marco said I wasn't ready.

I was getting to know the horses, but the one I still hadn't connected with was Carbine.

That horse was an asshole.

Footsteps sounded on the other side of my door in the hallway, and judging by their weight and speed, I knew it wasn't Dante. Conway and I hadn't spoken since his family left yesterday. I went to my room, and he went to his study.

I could admit my actions were a bit shady. I held his family as collateral because I knew he would rather die than let them know what was really going on between us. He made the mistake of telling me how close they were.

But it was the only leverage I had.

If I was going to spend a lifetime here, I didn't want to be an obedient slave.

I wanted to be a partner. Maybe I wouldn't be his girlfriend, but maybe I could be his friend. Maybe our sex would always be just sex, but at least it could be different now. At least everything could be different.

He walked in the door without knocking, still acting like he owned the damn place.

"Knock." My eyes shifted to his gaze, seeing the burning rage exploding inside him.

He stayed on the threshold and didn't move.

"Go back out and try it again."

He clenched his jaw so tightly it seemed like his eyes might pop out of his head. "I'll remember next time."

"No. Do it now."

He slammed the door shut behind him, solidifying his decision. "I'm not your bitch. Let's get that straight." He walked toward the bed, his thick arms rigid by his sides.

I shut my book and met his gaze, suddenly aware that we were alone together in my bedroom. Last time he fucked me, he gave it to me hard and good. There was no kissing or gentleness. And he didn't let me come.

I still hadn't forgiven him for it.

He stood right next to me, his piercing eyes billowing with a storm.

I didn't command him to leave and try knocking again. I knew his buttons had been pressed enough. "Yes?"

"I want sex."

I cocked an eyebrow, unable to believe those words really left his mouth. "And what do you want me to do about that?"

"Spread your legs. What else?"

I picked up my book and hit it against his chest. "No."

He didn't move despite the heaviness of the book. "I asked."

"Just because you asked doesn't mean you get it."

Both of his hands formed fists.

"And you didn't ask. You just came in here and spoke like a caveman."

"I'm liking this arrangement less and less…"

This wasn't a robotic relationship. He didn't just ask for something, and I fulfilled his desire. "If I were a woman in a bar, would you have said that?"

"Depends. Did I buy her for a hundred million dollars?" Both of his eyebrows furrowed.

I ignored what he said. "You would be nice to her. Buy her a drink. Flirt with her…not just blurt it out."

"You're telling me you want me to romance you?"

"I guess…maybe you could kiss me or touch me…get me in the mood."

He sighed. "You know how I feel about kissing."

"I know how you say you feel. But when you're kissing me, it sure seems like you enjoy it."

He stepped back from the bed and slid his hands into his pockets. "You said this was a compromise, but I feel like the only one making sacrifices here."

"Just treat me like a human being. Why is that so hard for you, Conway? I'm sure you've been with lots of women. You know how to get them into bed. Why can't you do that with me?"

"You think I buy them flowers and tell them they're beautiful and shit?" he snarled. "No, that's not what happens. Conway Barsetti gets pussy the second he walks into a room. Women throw themselves at me everywhere I go. I've never fucking swept a woman off her feet in my entire life, alright? I like it that way. It's ridiculous for you to expect to be any different."

"You bought me for a hundred million dollars…I have to be different."

He turned his gaze out the window, breathing through his rage. His chest rose and fell rapidly before he controlled it.

"How long do you expect to keep me, Conway?"

"Right now…I'm not sure."

"And you say I'm your fantasy, right?"

He slowly turned back to me, his eyes not quite so hostile.

"I can be your fantasy. But you need to be mine. That's what I'm asking."

He stared at me for a long time, never blinking his eyes.

"I want to feel beautiful. I want you to touch me gently. The first night we were together, you did everything I wanted. That's what I want all the time. I want you to treat me well. I want you to be a friend. When we first started working together, you were an ass sometimes…but you were also very sweet. That's what I want, Conway. If you start to treat me that way…I can be what you want. I'll make you feel wanted. I'll make you feel like a king. I'll say your name in bed or when your cock is in my mouth. I'll be what you want half the time, and you be what I want half the time. If this is a lifetime commitment, we should be what we need to each other."

He finally sat on the edge of my bed, his powerful muscles tense underneath his t-shirt. He rested his elbows on his knees and leaned forward. He stared out the window before he released a quiet sigh.

"Do you want to know about the first time I saw you?"

He finally blinked.

"I was sitting in a bar drinking scotch. I'd hit rock bottom, and there was a note from Knuckles sitting on the counter in front of me…"

He turned his gaze on me.

"An entertainment show was on TV, and they did a brief segment on you. They showed some pictures of you, talked about your fashion show, and showed a video of you before some award show…I thought you were the most handsome man I'd ever seen." Perhaps I should have kept that information to myself, but I decided to share it with him. This relationship would never change unless I made it change. "When I saw you in person, I thought the same thing. But then you opened your asshole mouth, and I realized you were too good to be true. You were harsh, arrogant, and rude. But that didn't change my attraction to you. When we have sex, I enjoy it. I try not to…but I do. I understand you don't want intimacy because it affects your work, but I'm asking you to make an exception for me. If I'm your fantasy, the inspiration for the greatest designs you've ever made, then perhaps I can inspire you even more. Perhaps if you take a chance, I can lead you to even greater success. I know there's a connection between us…you've felt it too."

He turned away when I finished speaking, rubbing his hands together as he stared out the window. He stared into the darkness before he shifted his gaze to his hands. Callused and corded, his hands belonged to a real man. His forearms were long and chiseled, and his biceps stretched his t-shirt. The lines of his body were so hard he seemed to be chiseled out of stone. "I don't like the idea, but I admit what we're doing now isn't working…"

"No, it isn't."

He continued to stare at his hands.

"I know you act like a bad guy sometimes, but I don't think you really are. I think you're a wonderful man, but you try to hide it to protect yourself. I think you have a heart, but you'll die before you let anyone go near it. I see it the most when you're with your family. If someone were to lay a single hand on your sister, you would murder him with your bare hands."

"Just because I love my sister doesn't mean I'm a good guy, Muse. Think about all the things I've done to you."

"And all of the things you've done for me…"

He looked out the window.

"I'm not saying you're perfect. You're complicated. That's fine. But I don't think you're as bad as you pretend to be. So stop pretending with me. You can be you when it's just the two of us."

He massaged his knuckles.

"We both know what would have happened to me if you didn't buy me."

"Yes. But I also just wanted to fuck you. I also wanted to be the one to take your virginity. So please stop rewriting history. Stop making me out to be some kind of hero. I'm not a hero, and I never want to be. Yes, it would be nice if you accepted me for who I was—the good, the bad, and the ugly. But don't pretend I'm something I'm not…that's annoying."

If that's what he wanted, I would drop it. "Can we try this, Conway?"

He didn't answer me.

I slid my hand across the bed and rested it on his arm.

He tensed at my touch.

I slid farther until I reached his fingers. I moved my hand between his and then finally grabbed him.

He didn't pull away.

I tightened my fingers between his.

He didn't respond. His body was immobile. He was lifeless. Then he released a quiet sigh and squeezed my hand. "Alright…we'll try."

———

CARBINE MOVED to the opposite side of the pen, his tail swishing about like he was irritated. The second I approached the fence, he developed this attitude. He didn't seem to like anyone, not even Marco. "I just washed and scrubbed these carrots. You're telling me you don't want them?"

He neighed and nibbled at the grass.

"You'd rather eat grass than this?" I asked incredulously.

Carbine ignored me altogether.

This horse had more sass than I did.

"He moves to the beat of his own drum." Conway approached me from behind, wearing brown boots, tight jeans, and a black t-shirt. His hands were in his pockets, and the scruff on his jaw made him look weathered like a man who really worked outdoors.

My heart immediately picked up when Conway drew near. Last night, we held hands for thirty minutes without speaking. It was the most intimacy we'd ever had, even more than the first time we were together.

Ever since that moment, it felt different.

"Then why do you keep him?"

He took one of the carrots from my hand. "He's a beautiful horse."

"But he doesn't like anyone."

"Not true." He rolled his tongue and released a loud whistle.

Carbine immediately lifted his head and looked toward Conway. Then he walked over, his footsteps increasing in pace the closer he got. His mane shifted in the breeze, like a snake crawling across a desert. He trotted to the fence and immediately smothered Conway with his breaths.

"Hey, boy." Conway scratched him behind the ear. "Is this

what you're after?" He held the carrot out, and Carbine devoured it. But once the food was gone, the horse stayed right along the fence with Conway.

I stood in shock. I'd never seen Carbine do anything but ignore Marco and me. But he clearly loved Conway. "I've never seen him act that way."

He rubbed him along his neck. "He and I just understand each other. Give him the carrot."

"Uh…he might bite my hand off."

"He won't. He's got an attitude, but he's not mean."

I held out the carrot, and Carbine ate it. He wasn't hostile toward me, but it was obvious he was only there to see Conway.

Conway rubbed him for a few more minutes before he rested his arms on the fence. "He's a beautiful stallion. I used to let people breed their mares with him, but I stopped."

"Why?"

He shrugged. "I felt wrong pimping him out."

"Well, maybe the reason he's so irritated is because he's not getting any action."

Conway chuckled. "He gets action with the mares sometimes. We usually sell those horses."

"Do you ever ride him?" He seemed too volatile to be controlled.

"I haven't in a while, but yes, I do."

"Does he try to buck you off?"

"No."

When Carbine stopped getting attention, he started to chomp on the grass again. His large lips pulled back as his teeth nibbled the short stalks. We stood together and watched him, the warm breeze moving across our skin.

Conway looked good in jeans that tight.

"How're the stables today?"

"Good. It doesn't seem to matter how much work I do, there's always more waiting for me the next day. It's impossible for it to be perfect for even a few days. Always requires attention."

"I can imagine."

"But I enjoy it. I was actually wondering how you'd feel about getting ponies…"

"Why would I do that?" His eyes were focused on Carbine.

"Because they're cute…"

When he turned back to me, he was smiling with his eyes. "I'm not interested in cute things."

"What if I took care of them?"

"What purpose would they serve?"

"What purpose do the horses serve?" I countered.

The corner of his mouth rose in a smile. "Good point."

"So…?"

"I'll think about it."

"We have the space. And we already have the feed and everything…it's not like it's that much of a hassle."

"Wow, you really want one, huh?"

"Well, it would have to be at least two. Having just one is cruel…they need a friend."

"I'll think about it," he repeated.

I stopped staring at Conway and looked at Carbine again. "What were you doing today?"

"I went to the studio for a few hours and met with Nicole. Those pieces I displayed have sold out a few times. She says I should start planning my next release. I have to strike while the iron is hot…"

"Not a bad idea. Do you have any thoughts planned?"

"A few," he said vaguely.

I glanced at the sun to see what time it was since I didn't have a watch. It was between three and four, and I had a few things to finish before the day was through. "I should get back to work."

He straightened at the fence, returning his arms to his sides. "Will you have dinner with me tonight?"

Despite the summer heat, I felt goose bumps sprinkle across my arms. "Sure."

"Great. I'll see you then."

WE SAT on the terrace with a single white candle between us. Dante prepared juicy steaks with stalks of asparagus along with a side of potatoes. He selected the wine to complement the food, and we had a five-star meal right in the backyard.

The sun had set thirty minutes ago, and now a faint line stretched over the horizon. Splashes of blue, orange, and pink mixed with the clouds that started to roll in as the temperature cooled.

Conway and I didn't say much. Ever since we came to our agreement, we spoke to each other less. There was simply less to say since he wasn't bossing me around all the time. The basis of our relationship was fighting back and forth. Without it, there wasn't much to go on.

But I preferred the quiet over arguing.

He stared at me most of the time, his black shirt showing off the thickness of his arms. He'd shaved before dinner, so his jaw was clean of the stubble he had earlier that afternoon. His eyes were dark like his shirt, giving him a look of constant shadow. The only time he pulled his gaze away was to look at his steak as he cut off a piece.

I was getting used to his stares. The look was identical to

what it used to be, but it somehow felt different. "Was Vanessa's story true? You really did that?"

He sipped his wine before he answered. "Yes."

"Why?"

"Men are disgusting assholes—that's why."

"Yes, but not all of them are."

He shook his head. "Yes, all. Of all women, you should agree with that statement."

I couldn't when an exception was sitting right across from me. But since he hated being labeled as a good guy, I didn't tell him that. "Do you look after her a lot?"

"A lot more than she thinks. She got upset with me when I followed her, but she thinks that's the first time. The fact that she's never noticed me before concerns me."

"She seems like a capable young woman."

"She's not. She's young and naïve. She thinks the world is a beautiful place and she needs a blank canvas to capture it all. Fucking annoying."

"Sounds like she has a good spirit."

"She does. I wouldn't be so concerned if she weren't so damn beautiful." He sighed before he took another drink of his wine. "I'm her brother, and even I can't pretend she's ugly. Anytime I'm out with her, all the men stare at her. But I can't strangle twelve men at one time, so I just have to deal with it. So how many men stare at her when she's by herself?"

"She may be ignorant, but I doubt she's ignorant to that. Every beautiful woman knows what it's like to be stared at."

"But not every woman understands she's not invincible. Vanessa has a false sense of self. She thinks she's stronger than she really is. If someone grabs her, she thinks she'll be able to fight them off…but she can't."

His deep concern for his sister made me wonder if there was more to the story than he was telling me. "Conway, did something happen?"

It was the first time he'd dropped his gaze during the conversation. "Meaning?"

"You and your father both seemed…uncomfortable by the topic."

He drank his wine again, this time taking a much bigger sip. "I'd rather not talk about it."

So there was a reason. "I'm sorry I asked."

He finished his glass and refilled it. "When she decided she wanted to study in Milan, it was difficult for my parents to let her go. They've protected her her entire life. Since she's close to me, I feel the need to look after her. So far there haven't been any issues, but you never know. A part of me wants her to marry a very powerful man, that way I'll never have to worry about her ever again."

"Maybe she will."

He shook his head. "She's too independent and has way too much sass. She scares men away."

"A truly good man won't be scared away. So, when she meets the right one, he'll stick around."

"Maybe."

I adjusted the sleeves of my dress. I was wearing the dress that Dante had brought to my room, light blue with a deep plunge down the front. The neckline was so low I couldn't wear a bra with it, so I'd taped my nipples down so they wouldn't press through the thin fabric. "I think it's sweet that you care about her so much. I can tell she loves you."

"Because she has to."

"No…definitely not."

He looked across the fields at the land in the distance. Judging by his coldness, the subject had officially expired. "I don't know anything about your family. What were they like?"

"My father died a really long time ago. Car accident. My mother followed him a few years later when she got sick. I have an aunt that lives in California, but I've never been close to her. Nathan was all I had…until I realized who he really was."

"I'm sorry."

I didn't have a close family the way Conway did. Even

when my parents were alive, we were never close. When my brother and I lived under the same roof, we didn't spend much time together. Maybe if we had, I would have realized what was going on. If I weren't so focused on myself, maybe I would have been able to help him.

"You don't like to talk about this. I'm sorry I asked."

I hadn't realized how well Conway could read me until then. "There's something I'd like to know."

"Yes?"

"When you first saw me…what were you thinking?" I knew what I was thinking when I first saw him, and I'd even shared that moment with him. Would he share that moment with me?

"I wasn't thinking anything."

I didn't believe that was possible, so I stared at him and waited for more.

"I just saw you, and I finally stopping thinking." He kept his eyes on the horizon. "In my world, my mind is always going a million miles an hour. I'm constantly wondering what I should do next, what model will complement my next piece. But when I saw you…I stopped thinking altogether. It was so quiet. You were the answer I wasn't looking for. You were the perfect model I never thought I would find. It was so true, so real, I didn't need to think about anything at all."

I felt my pulse quicken in my neck, felt the vein tremble. My breathing increased slightly, remembering the sight of his silhouette in that dark auditorium. The fact that I made this brilliant man stop thinking made me understand the true impact I had on him.

"And ever since that moment…you've been my star."

It made me wonder if he'd felt that way about other models before me. Did I replace Lacey Lockwood? Did she replace someone before her? "Do you feel that way about models often?"

He turned back to me, his eyes narrowed. "Never."

"Just me…?"

He nodded. "I've never laid eyes on a more beautiful woman. When I told you that, I meant it."

When he was kind like this, it was hard for me not to like him. And I didn't just like him because he was such a beautiful man. I liked him because there was so much more to him. He could make me feel so pretty so easily. "Did you sleep with Lacey Lockwood?"

His eyes narrowed. "What does that have to do with anything?"

"I'm just wondering if you regularly sleep with your models."

"Who I sleep with is none of your business," he said coldly.

I swallowed the insult and knew I'd spoiled the night by asking the question, even though that was never my intention. Since we were sleeping together, I'd thought the conversation was appropriate.

Conway closed his eyes and sighed, probably realizing his reply was ice-cold. "No, I've never slept with her. I don't sleep with my models."

I couldn't hide my surprise at the revelation. I felt my eyebrows lift. "What?"

He did his best to fight the irritation that burned in his eyes. "You heard what I said."

"But…I'm surprised by that."

"I don't mix business with pleasure."

"You're sleeping with me."

"And that's why you aren't one of my models anymore. Now you're just my inspiration, my private fantasy."

"The girls seem so infatuated with you…and that lipstick on your neck…I just assumed."

"The second I sleep with them, everything would get complicated. This way, their rank is based solely on merit. There's no chance of jealousy when I won't fuck any of them. I can get ass just as hot off the runway."

I didn't like to picture him getting ass from anyone, although I wasn't sure why. "So that lipstick really wasn't from sleeping with someone?"

He held my gaze and didn't flinch. "No. Like I said, I haven't slept with anyone."

"But you intend to?"

He paused before he answered the question. "I already explained that to you."

I could coerce him into monogamy, but that might make him lie about it. I preferred honesty.

"Are you finished?" he asked.

"Yes. It was delicious."

We left the table and returned to the house. After two flights of stairs, we were in the hallway where our bedrooms were located.

He was making an effort to treat me the way I wanted to be treated. I knew I should give him what he wanted in return. After spending an evening across from him looking so sexy in that t-shirt, the idea didn't sound bad.

It sounded nice, actually.

I couldn't believe I'd waited so long to get laid—it was pretty damn incredible.

He stopped in front of my doorway, his eyes focused on my lips.

I knew what would happen next. I pressed my hands against his chest and moved into him, my lips aiming for his. He wanted to skip the kissing, but it was my favorite part. I loved feeling his mouth against mine. It was when I felt most connected to him.

I kissed him.

He kissed me back.

I kept the kiss soft and short. My fingers felt the hardness of his body, and I breathed into his mouth, thinking about the way his large cock felt inside me. It used to hurt, but now I loved how full he made me feel.

I pulled my mouth away and dropped my hands. "Get in bed. I'll be there in a second."

His eyes immediately darkened when he realized he was getting what he wanted.

"I just want to fix myself up a bit…"

"Top drawer."

"Sorry?"

"There's lingerie in your top drawer." He turned his back to me and walked into his bedroom. The door clicked audibly behind him, but he didn't turn around to look at me again.

Now my heart was beating so fast. My palms were searing hot but frozen at the same time. I walked into my bedroom and opened the top drawer to discover the dozens of selections. Different fabrics and different colors, every piece was sexy in a unique way. The first one I grabbed had so many strings I wasn't sure how it worked, so I grabbed the one underneath it. A silver lace bodysuit with a fastened crotch, it was the next choice in the pile. I assumed they were sorted by preference, so I pulled it on.

I'd done this before so I shouldn't feel nervous, but it felt like the first time all over again. The last time I was in his bedroom, he peeled the white lingerie off my body and took away my innocence. I slept beside him all night, his strong arms wrapped around me. It was a nice memory… despite the circumstances.

I walked into his suite in the silver heels I found in my closet and made my way toward his bedroom. My pace was sluggish because I was nervous. We were operating our relationship differently, and something about that made me uneasy. I didn't know what to expect. The fact that I wanted him while sitting across from him at dinner all night made me wonder if I'd lost my mind. I had the power to refuse him as much as I wanted, but I didn't want to refuse him at all.

I wanted to get into that bed with him.

Like I was on the runway, I straightened my body and held my head high. My shoulders were back, my collarbone was prominent, and my tummy was tucked toward my spine. My heels echoed lightly against the hardwood floor, so he could hear my approach as easily as I could.

I wanted to be his fantasy, to give him the kind of experience he craved most. It was difficult for me to do that since I had so little practice. Whenever he came into my bedroom for sex, it was usually face-to-face and his cock was deep inside me.

The door was open so I crossed into his bedroom.

His fireplace was lit, casting a golden light across the bed. He sat upright against the wooden headboard, his massive shoulders stretching from one side to the next. His tanned skin glowed in the light, and the shadows separating his muscles were dark and exaggerated. He turned his head slightly to look at me, his hands resting on the covers that were pulled up to his waist. All of his clothes were scattered across the floor, so I knew he was naked under there.

I couldn't wait to see for myself.

I walked to the edge of the bed then slipped off my left heel.

"Keep the heels on."

I flinched before I pulled it back on. I straightened again before I looked at him, unsure what to do. Did I climb on top of him? Did I strip for him? Did I crawl up his body and start sucking his cock?

I wasn't sure.

But I knew I had to stop overthinking it. Instead of concentrating on what I thought he wanted, I just went with my instincts. Men liked sex, regardless of what position it was. And they wanted a woman to want them. All I had to do was that, and it should be good enough.

I crawled onto the bed and moved on top of him, my legs straddling his hips. I lowered myself and sat right on his hard cock, all nine inches of his thickness. It was warm to the touch, even through the lace that separated us.

His hands started at my knees and slightly migrated up my thighs toward my hips. He pressed his fingers into me with a bit of pressure, and his eyes followed his movement. Up, up, he went, moving over my belly until he secured his hands around my ribcage. Then he flicked his eyes up to mine.

He looked so sexy with the back of his head resting against the headboard. He was aroused but in a lazy way. His cock twitched slightly underneath me, the gentle pulsing hitting me right against my clit. He looked into my eyes with confidence, like he knew I wanted to be there as much as he did.

He slid his hands around my waist and slowly they moved to my ass. My bodysuit was a thong, so my cheeks were bare to his touch. He kneaded them with his fingertips, gripping my cheeks and massaging them.

Once I stopped thinking about my situation and operated based on my emotions, my heartbeat slowed down, and my hands immediately moved on their own. They held on to both of his shoulders for balance, and I leaned in to kiss his full lips.

He kissed me back immediately, this time with no reluctance.

I took a deep breath the instant I felt him, the chemistry hotter than last time. He turned his head slightly and gently pulled my bottom lip into his mouth. He kissed me a little harder before he closed his mouth and opened it again. He guided me in a sexy dance with our lips, our bodies moving together slowly and our mouths devouring one another.

His hands gripped my cheeks harder, and he scooted me

even closer toward him, drawing my tits against his hard chest. He massaged my ass harder, his fingertips exploring me deeper than before. I could feel his chest rise with every breath he took, feel the excitement as his pulse started to pick up.

The sexy sounds our mouths made filled the room, louder than the distant fireplace on the other side of the room. The quietness was one of the sexiest aspects of the moment because we could listen to every reaction we had for each other.

His hand slipped into my hair next, and he pulled it away from my face, his kiss growing deeper and harder. He moved his lips to the corner of my mouth then sprinkled kisses along my jawline, slowly moving to my neck. Then he kissed me everywhere, laying his mouth across my shoulders as he gripped my hair tighter. He secured his arm around my waist and tugged me closer to him, his heavy breaths filling my ear canal.

Now I wasn't thinking at all.

I was just touching him, kissing him, feeling him. I didn't think about the past or why I was there. I didn't think about our new agreement or what I was running from. Right now, I was just a woman who wanted a man. I was just a woman spending the night with the sexiest and richest lingerie designer in the world.

His mouth trailed back to mine, and he kissed me again, this time more aggressively than before. His fingers dug into me whenever he gripped me, clawing at my body like he couldn't get enough.

My hands explored his hard chest, feeling the hammering of his strong heart. He was just as excited as I was, unbridled like a wild horse.

He sucked my bottom lip into his mouth as he reached between my legs and unfastened the fabric with the quick movements of his thumb and forefinger. It immediately came undone, and the bodysuit bunched up toward my waist.

He moved two fingers over my entrance then moaned into my mouth when he felt the pool of liquid drip onto his hand. He rubbed his fingers and thumb together, his lips still pressed to mine. "Jesus…"

It was the first time I didn't feel ashamed of the way I felt about him. My pussy was aching to feel his enormous cock inside me. I wanted to experience that stretching now that it felt so good. I was immensely attracted to this man, not just because of his appearance, but his dedication to his work and his obvious self-respect. Not to mention, he was so powerful that even a terrifying man like Knuckles backed off. "I want you, Conway."

He ended the kiss and stared into my eyes instead, his expression cold and hot at the same time. His jaw was hard, and the fire cast a thick shadow along his mouth. His full lips were pressed together, and his eyebrows were furrowed in the sexiest way. "You mean that, Muse?"

I didn't expect him to ask that because it didn't seem

important. Whether I really wanted him or not, he shouldn't care. He'd bought me to enjoy. Like he said, I was just a toy he used for his own amusement.

I guided his hand to my body, pressing his fingers against the slickness oozing from between my legs. "You can't tell?"

He pressed his forehead against mine and released a quiet moan, the sound coming from deep within his throat. His fingers dug into me harder, practically bruising the skin with his enthusiasm.

I rose above him and then grabbed him by the shaft. It was the first time I'd ever pressed him into me, the first time I'd actually initiated the act of sex. I felt his crown push against my entrance, getting smeared in my lubrication.

He moaned the second he felt me, his eye locked on to mine.

I slowly sank down, inching him deeper inside me as I lowered myself toward his waist. Even though my body had finally been broken in, he was simply too large for my petiteness. It was difficult to get him inside, so I had to take it slow, moving inch by inch. When he was halfway inside, I moaned at his intrusion. He took up all of me. If he were any bigger, this just wouldn't work.

He grabbed my hips and directed me the rest of the way down, slowly guiding me until he was balls deep inside me. "Fucking perfect." He was eye level with me as he rested his back against the headboard. He grabbed the fabric bunched around my waist and pulled it over my head so he could palm my tits with his big hands. Aggressively, he squeezed them. When he flicked his thumb over the nipple, he did it roughly, making me pebble and ache. "Fuck me, Muse." He moved his hands to my ass and pulled me up, providing guidance since I'd never done this before. He arched my back as he pulled me forward. When he pushed back, he had my back bend in a different direction.

The result was an incredible stimulation of my clit against his pelvic bone. The thickness of his cock set my nerves on fire, and I felt full of him in every way imaginable. I moved slowly because I could barely handle how good it felt. This beautiful man was pleasing me, when I was the one trying to please him.

He closed his eyes and sighed under his breath. "Muse…" He guided me up and down slowly, as if any increase in pace would ruin him. His fingers dug into my ass every time he yanked on me. His chest expanded with the deep breaths he took, and his jaw clenched tighter than ever before. That concentrated expression stretched across his face, similar to the one he wore when he was focused on creating something. But this expression was a million times more intense.

Just that would make me come. "Conway…"

He wrapped his hand around my neck and pulled me into him for a kiss. He kissed me slowly as he moved his hips into me, his big cock slowly sliding in and out of my body.

One hand stayed on my ass while the other gripped my neck.

His kiss was always my undoing. I loved feeling his breath enter my lungs. I loved feeling his fingertips press directly into my neck. His kisses were always purposeful, as if he were trying to enjoy every single exchange of our lips. I felt like the only woman in his life when we were together like this. He never kissed anyone, but he made an exception for me. That made me feel special.

My lips began to tremble, and my nails dug into his shoulders. "You're going to make me come…" It was the first time I didn't try to fight it. Now, I waited anxiously for it, knowing it was going to be a cosmic explosion. My breath came out shaky, and my body tightened in preparation. His cock was hitting me in the perfect spot, grinding up against my walls in the most stimulating way.

He kissed the corner of my mouth and breathed with me. "I'll always make you come, Muse." He guided my hips up and down as he thrust into me, increasing the pace and making us both sweat.

I hit the finish line and came all over him, screaming in his face and digging my nails into his flesh. "Conway…" My pussy tightened around his length, squeezing him with crushing force. The climax was better than any other I'd experienced, probably because I wanted this one.

"Fuck…come all over my dick."

I felt the pool of moisture slather his dick once my pussy

finally stopped contracting. I clung to him harder as I finished the remaining high, hugging him with unexpected tightness. I buried my face in his neck because I didn't know what else to do. Overcome with the sensation wreaking havoc inside me, I was a prisoner to everything I was feeling.

He wrapped his arms around me and squeezed me as he continued to thrust into me. His skin was searing hot, and his grip was tight. He breathed with me, enjoying my orgasm as much as I did.

When it finally passed, I continued to cling to him as the sensation slowly drifted away. There was a line of sweat down the center of my shoulder blades. My skin was hot from the exertion as well as his touch. It took me a moment to recover from the thrill, and I slowly sat back with his entire dick inside me.

His face was flushed with a tint of pink, the vein in his forehead throbbing. He gripped my waist with his fingers, and he pressed his face between my tits. He licked the sweat in the valley and then sucked each of my nipples.

I rested my chin on his head as I dug my fingers into his hair. "Come inside me, Conway."

He moaned with my tit in his mouth. "You're fucking unbelievable." He pulled his head back and rested against the headboard again. Then he dragged me up and down his length, fucking me at a quick speed. He pressed his feet against the sheets as he thrust his hips up into me.

I held on to his shoulders as I rocked back, taking his

length as he gave it to me. I could feel him thicken inside me, feel his cock prepare for the big explosion.

He grabbed my hand and twisted it behind me so I could cup his balls with my fingertips.

I massaged his sac, my nails gently roaming over his textured skin as I moved up and down on his dick.

He gripped my hips and gave his final thrusts before he exploded, filling me with all of his seed. "Yes..." He pulled me harder onto his length, getting every inch inside me to give me everything he had. He rested the back of his head against the wood as he stared at me, his eyes focused with deadly intensity.

I could feel him fill me, feel his seed expand inside me. It was warm and heavy, and there was even more than there'd ever been before. It took his cock a few seconds before it started to soften. The fullness started to dwindle as the satisfaction replaced it.

I maneuvered off of him slowly to make sure his come wouldn't spill anywhere. I rolled over and lay on my back, feeling his come sit inside me. My sweat immediately clung to the sheets, and I closed my eyes as the relaxation swept over me. I'd never felt so at peace, so satisfied. If sex was always that great, then I felt idiotic for waiting so long.

Conway remained still when the sex was over. His back was still to the headboard, and his wet dick lay against his hard stomach.

I turned my head toward him and watched him.

His eyes were lidded, but they weren't closed. He looked just as tired as I was, fully satisfied by my performance.

I didn't clean up because I knew he wanted me to keep his come inside me. He wanted me to sleep with his seed inside me all night. I turned on my side and closed my eyes, feeling myself slip away almost immediately.

"Muse."

His deep voice made my eyes snap open again. I must have fallen asleep slightly because his voice was jarring. "Hmm?"

He leaned over me and pressed a kiss to my hairline. "You should go to bed before you get too tired."

"I am in bed." I opened my eyes and looked into his handsome face, seeing his pretty green eyes.

His hand moved over my tummy. "I mean in your own bed…" He kept his voice gentle to soften the blow. In the beginning, I didn't understand what he meant. But now, I understood it perfectly. He must have sensed my feeling of rejection because he leaned down and kissed the corner of my mouth. "I'm not trying to be an ass…"

Since I knew exactly what it was like when he was being an asshole, I knew that was the truth. "You let me sleep in here before."

He rubbed his nose against mine. "You know why, Muse."

Something about his bed was so comfortable. It must be the sheets or the mattress. Or maybe it was the strong man beside me. In this large mansion, I felt safe behind the solid walls and the gate around the property. But I felt even safer when he was beside me. It would be easy for me to get angry, but I knew Conway was giving his best effort to compromise with me. He'd done his best not to boss me around, and he'd done his best to treat me with the respect I asked for.

He gave me more of himself than he ever gave to anyone else.

I shouldn't push it. "Good night." I sat up and pulled my hair over one shoulder.

He leaned back so I could rise. "Good night."

I didn't want to pull the lingerie back on, especially since the bottoms were soaked with my arousal. I walked to his dresser and placed my hand on the knob. "Can I take a t-shirt?"

He got out of bed and walked to the bathroom, buck naked and beautiful. "Of course."

I pulled it over my head then walked to the door without any panties. I just needed to be covered until I got to my bedroom down the hall. It was unlikely I'd cross paths with anyone at this time of night, but I didn't want to risk it.

"Muse?"

I stopped in the doorway and looked at him.

His wide shoulders led to narrow hips. Past that, he had

muscular thighs and toned calves. He told me every single one of my features was perfect when most women just had a few perfect attributes. But he was exactly the same way. I'd never seen a man more masculine and more handsome at the same time. "Thank you."

I didn't know what he was thanking me for, so I waited for an explanation.

"Thank you for putting up with me."

4

Conway

I slept well the night before, so I woke up earlier than usual. I went for a run around the estate before I jumped into the pool to cool off. Dante was awake because he never allowed me to be awake earlier than he was, even if it was a Sunday. I had breakfast on the terrace before the sun even rose over the horizon.

My thoughts kept drifting back to the erotic night I'd had with Muse.

She'd crawled right into my lap without my asking. She rode me like it wasn't her first time, and she was so wet between her legs I nearly came before I was even inside her. There was kissing and touching, heavy breathing and moaning. She said my name and didn't resist the orgasm I gave her. It was definitely a fantasy, something so sexy I wasn't sure if it was real. I had the most gorgeous woman on my lap, and I felt her skin-on-skin. Her perfect tits were in my face, firm and delicious.

She really made me feel like a man.

Her inexperience aroused me even more. I'd been with women who were amazing lays, but they didn't compare to this innocent woman who was learning everything. I got to watch her realize what she enjoyed. I got to watch her explore her sexuality, watch her deal with her feelings for me.

It was sexy as hell.

Now my mind was buzzing with ideas. My fingers ached to feel the perfect fabric in my hands. I needed a needle and thread. I needed my Muse to stand there and inspire me, to channel all of my desire into the lingerie I would make for women everywhere.

After breakfast, I stopped by her room. I nearly stepped inside like last time, but then I remembered what I promised her. After what she did for me last night, I was more motivated to fulfill my end of the bargain. It was in my nature to storm into every room I owned and do whatever I wanted. I was a naturally bossy and aggressive man who cared little about the way other people felt. But Muse forced me to be more polite…despite my aversion to politeness. I tapped my knuckles against the wood.

It was barely seven in the morning so it was early, but since she headed out to the stables every day, she was probably going to wake up soon anyway. Her quiet voice reached me. "Come in."

I opened the door and stepped inside.

She sat up in bed and turned on her bedside lamp. With messy hair and sleepy eyes, she covered her mouth and yawned. The covers fell back slightly, revealing her in the t-shirt she took from my dresser. "Did you need something?" She looked at the alarm clock on the nightstand and squinted her eyes to read the time.

I sat on the edge of the bed and looked at her with a soft smile, finding her cute first thing in the morning. Her makeup was gone, and now her skin glowed after a good night of rest. Her eyes shone a little brighter than normal, probably because they were rested too. "I'm going to the studio in Milan today. I'd like you to come with me."

"What are you doing?"

"Designs."

She probably wanted to stay behind and work in the stables, but since we were both compromising, she wouldn't defy me. Using her for inspiration was one of the reasons I bought her in the first place. It wouldn't be right if she denied me—and she knew that. "Let me shower and have some breakfast."

"We're leaving in an hour."

"That should be enough time."

A part of me wanted to pull back the covers and crawl between her legs. Morning sex was always nice. The second I opened my eyes, my dick was usually hard against my stomach. Having soft lips wrap around him would be better than a fresh cup of coffee—any day. But

I'd rather save it for later. "Meet me in my room when you're ready."

I DROVE my red Ferrari from Verona to Milan. It was only an hour trip, but riding in this car cut the time in half. I'd had women sit in the passenger seat many times, but never one so beautiful.

This car was made for me.

Muse stared out the window and enjoyed the sights with an appreciative eye. To her, this world was beautiful and new. Since I grew up in this gorgeous country, I took it for granted. My backyard was one of the most spectacular and historic places in the world. "Which part of Italy is your favorite?"

"Tough question."

She sat back against the leather seat and turned to me. "Life is all about tough questions."

I chuckled. "I love the heat of the south. The vineyards, hillsides, and wine…all of it. It doesn't snow there, so the winters are mild. But Milan is a very progressive city. Life is a little quicker here. It's home to many designers and fashion icons. I find it inspiring."

"Okay…you told me why you love two different places. Now pick one."

"Why do I have to pick just one?" I asked incredulously. "All of Italy is beautiful."

"Because I like to make you squirm."

I'd spent nearly all my adult life in Milan so I considered it my home, but my roots were unforgettable. "If I had to choose…I prefer the south. My parents have a beautiful property, and we're surrounded by vineyards in the hillsides. My uncle lives just a mile away, and the main winery my family runs is right down the road."

"So you were in the country the way you are now?"

"Yes…but it's different."

"Do your parents have horses?"

Talking about my parents left a twinge of annoyance in my chest. They believed in a ridiculous lie that Muse made up. Now I'd have to go along with it…for god knows how long. "No."

"Then why did your father buy you a horse?"

How did she know that? "Did Marco tell you that?"

She tensed in alarm. "Yeah…I was curious why you had such an ornery horse."

"He's not ornery," I said. "He just doesn't like you."

"Or Marco," she countered. "You seem to be the only person he does like."

"Like I said, we understand each other. And my father

bought me a horse because he said the horse reminded him of me. I had the stables at the time, so he brought him over. My father doesn't want to deal with the time and effort of keeping up horses, even though he's the hardest working person I know. So he brought one over here."

"That's nice." She looked out the window again.

I kept my eyes on the road with one hand on the wheel. I hoped the conversation about my family was over. They were the only things in the world that actually mattered to me, besides my career and my wealth. But having something important in my life made it dangerous. If someone wanted something from me, it would be easy to coerce me. "I spent some time in the neighboring villages while I was waiting for your audition. I slept under the stars at night, and even though I had no money, people would give me food. I didn't even need to beg. They just said I was too thin…"

The idea of her walking through Italy completely homeless made a rock form in my stomach. She had been unsafe and unprotected. A beautiful woman like her should be shielded from the evils of this world. It was the reason I wanted Vanessa to marry a big, perfect man. If he loved her, he would protect her every single minute of the day—and she would allow him to.

"Italians are very generous and kind. In America, that wouldn't have happened. People would have just called the police and had me moved."

"You shouldn't have been out there alone."

"I didn't have any other choice. There were a few hostels around, so I took advantage of that, but they don't let you stay for long."

I didn't want to talk about this anymore. It made my blood boil. "Dante seems to be warming up to you."

"You think?" she asked. "I just accept his food and never lift a finger. I don't even say much to him."

"All he wants is to wait on you. If you allow him to, he perks up."

"He shouldn't have to do everything. I'm perfectly capable."

I shrugged. "It gives him joy. Just like how Marco doesn't understand why you would be shoveling horse shit in the stables when you could be lying by the pool all day. Doesn't make much sense to me either, honestly."

"Well, I can't sit around all the time. Just how Dante can't work all the time."

I could retire if I wanted to, but I loved my work too much. I supposed it was hypocritical of me to challenge her like that. "So you still like the stables?"

"Yeah. Marco said I'm still not ready to ride…I'm not sure if I'll ever be."

I told him she wasn't allowed because it was too dangerous. So he made up excuses for me. "Why do you want to ride so much?"

"Why?" she asked incredulously. "Lots of people love to ride horses. It's a great hobby."

"It's a lot of work and can be dangerous."

"But if you're always careful, it should be fine."

There was no point in arguing with her. She was stubborn—just like me.

We drove into Milan and arrived at the building I owned. It had once been a historical landmark, and I bought it before they had the chance to tear it down. I never did any reconstruction to the outside because I loved the architecture, but the inside had been redone to fit my needs.

Muse and I walked inside.

The models were located on the second floor, where they had a private gym, their wardrobe, and workout classes. It also held the changing room and the studio where photos were taken.

We took the stairs and spotted a few girls dressed in the lingerie I'd released for the show a few weeks ago.

"Conway." Veronica had one hand on her hip and walked up to me with her heels clapping against the hardwood floor. The teal fabric looked great on her dark skin. Her belly button was pierced, a bright jewel shining. "Long time, no see." She leaned into me, grabbed me by the bicep, and pressed a kiss to my cheek.

"Veronica, you look beautiful." I kissed her on the cheek in reciprocation.

Juliet came up to me and did the same, a blonde in black lingerie. "Everyone is loving your designs. Are you working on your next release?"

"Actually, yes. I'm sure you'll be impressed." I turned to the stairs to move to the third floor.

Muse faltered for a moment before she followed me.

The girls were warm to me, but they gave her looks of pure loathing.

I knew exactly how women were, so I kept walking up the stairs. Nicole told me about all the fights that she broke up between the models, the envy the women had for each other. They usually didn't turn physical, but they still played dirty. They would cut off large chunks of hair when a girl's back was turned, or they would sprinkle bulk powder in their smoothies to make them gain weight.

I had more important things to do, so I ignored it.

Muse trailed behind me then reached my side once we were on the third floor. She was quiet, brooding, and hostile, and her disappointment was heavy in the air around me.

I ignored it and stepped inside the studio. Everything had been organized by Nicole, who was the only person allowed to touch my things. She was the only person who knew exactly how I liked to keep my materials. She made sure nothing was lost or misplaced.

I flicked on the lights and peeled off my jacket. The sun filtering through the windows was hot that morning, and the collared shirt and tie were already warm enough. Nicole had imported the fabric samples I asked for, and they were spread out across my work table. I felt each one with my fingertips.

Muse stood with her arms over her chest, her frown deep.

I continued to ignore it. "It'll be difficult for me to top my last line of lingerie, so I'm not going to chase that success again. I'm going in a different direction."

She stayed on the other side of the table, her silence louder than words.

"Watching you in the stables gave me some ideas." I opened my notebook and glanced at the sketches.

Muse remained as hostile as ever.

"Remove your clothes." I kept my eyes on the paper, and when I didn't hear any movement, I looked up to meet her gaze.

She wore a fiery expression. "Excuse me?"

The second I stepped into my office, I'd reverted back to my old ways. It was a habit that would be difficult to break. "Please."

She remained rigid, defiant even though I'd corrected myself.

I knew what this was really about. "I said I don't sleep with my models. No reason to be jealous."

"I'm not jealous."

"Really?" I challenged. "Because you've been in a pissed mood ever since we ran into Veronica and Juliet."

"I just don't see why you need to kiss everyone all the time."

"Don't insult my culture."

"Your culture?" she snapped. "So if I kissed every handsome man I saw, you'd be perfectly okay with that?"

When Carter tried to take a picture of her ass, I nearly knocked him out. I didn't like anyone looking at my muse, and if anyone touched her, I'd bury them six feet under. If her full lips ever touched another man's skin, I'd explode. "It's different."

"Different because it's sexist."

"I'm not sexist." I never judged a woman for taking off her clothes. I never thought less of a woman for having several partners. I didn't think they were less intelligent just because they used their bodies to make their rent. As the son of a strong woman and a respectful man, I was raised in accordance with their values.

"Seems that way."

I gripped the edge of the wood as I stared at her across the table. "I understand we're trying to have an equal relationship, but let's not forget the foundation of this arrangement. I own you—end of story."

"It's not the end of the story, Conway."

"I kiss my models because it's part of my image. They

look to me for guidance. They look to me for protection. I take care of my girls. If a man disrespects them in my presence, one of my men breaks their spine. Since I don't sleep with them, there's nothing for you to be upset about."

"But they all want to sleep with you."

They made moves on me all the time, but I wouldn't get into that. "Doesn't matter what they want." I turned back to my sketches. "Now, let's get to work."

She still didn't move.

My eyes flicked back up to her. "I've asked you politely twice now. I won't do it again, Muse."

She finally dropped her arms to her sides and removed her clothing. She stripped down to her thong and bra, standing in the room like she was ready for the runway. She used to be so uncomfortable standing in there with me. But now, it was like being at home.

I stood in front of her and examined her, thinking of the distance between different parts of her body. My hands started at her shoulders, and I pressed into her, touching her frame intimately. I knew her body so well because I'd tasted it, worshiped it. But I wanted to feel it more, feel her perfect measurements before I began. "Your complexion…is so stunning." My thumb rubbed against her shoulder. "The color is beautiful. There's no color fabric that won't complement it. It's not too dark or too light."

She stared at me, her features slack. "Thanks…I guess."

I grabbed her chin and directed her to look up, straining the muscles in her neck. "I have an idea. Stay there." I grabbed a few pieces of black fabric and held them against her skin. I switched them out, looking for the perfect color and texture to showcase exactly what I wanted. When it came to the perfect model, I needed the perfect design. Anything less than flawless simply wasn't good enough.

Once I found the exact dark fabric that would complement her skin the best, I rolled the fabric to the table and started to work.

She continued to stand there. "Can I put my clothes back on?"

"There's a robe on the hanger over there," I said without looking up from what I was doing.

She didn't put it on, and I knew exactly why.

"I designed that robe for you. No one else has worn it."

Her footsteps echoed on the floor as she retrieved it. She wrapped it around her body and tied the sash across her stomach. She came over to me next, the smell of her shampoo entering my nose once she was close enough. "Can I help?"

"No." I did everything alone. The only person who helped me was Nicole. She did all the bookkeeping and the ordering. Everything else was my responsibility.

She sighed beside me. "You paid a lot for me. May as well get the most use out of me…"

"I bought you so I could fuck you." I looked up and stared into her eyes. "Do you want me to fuck you, Muse?" I was immersed in my work, but I'd always make an exception for this woman.

She held my gaze, no longer intimidated by my stare. "Maybe later." She grabbed my sketchbook and pulled the drawing closer to her. She examined it, turning it slightly sideways to take it in at a different angle. She examined the lines of fabric over the shoulders and the stomach. It was a one-piece design, but it was composed of thin straps everywhere, making it a complicated piece, but very beautiful. "Wow…I really like this. How did you come up with it?"

"You."

"But how?" she asked. "Was it something I wore? Something I did? I don't wear anything like this in the stables."

"No." I turned the page back toward me. "But the lines represent ropes. I've seen you down there a few times, pulling the horses or organizing the reins. And seeing you hold the ropes made me think about what I would do to you with the ropes." I pictured her wrists bound together behind her back as she rode me. Powerless to do anything, she would be mine to enjoy. I'd be the cowboy, and she'd be the bronco. I turned my eyes to hers, unashamed by what I said. "It'll be in black and brown, resembling the color and texture of rope. Every man wants to tie up a woman. Now the woman can tie herself up…" I turned back to my work and organized the fabric before I cut it.

She remained beside me, her fingertips resting on the paper. "Do you think about tying me up?"

I cut the first sheet of fabric. "Yes."

"But you haven't."

"I figured we would take things slow…since you're new to all of this." I'd never considered myself to be a patient man, but when it came to Muse, my entire agenda was based on her timetable.

She took the line of fabric and held it in her fingertips. "What's this go to?"

"The first strap."

"I'd like to help, Conway. I may have no experience with clothes, but I'm a fast learner."

The more time I spent with her, the more I understood her personality. She liked to be active, to do things constantly rather than sit around all day. My father was the exact same way, and she reminded me of him. She reminded me of my mother too. But with my mom, she'd always been a full-time parent to us. That was her job as well as her hobby. "Alright. Here's the measurement." I pushed the measurement table toward her. "Cut it to this precise size."

"Okay."

I turned back to what I was doing, and every time I finished one part, I handed it off to her for the next step. I was surprised she did it correctly, and I realized it cut my time in half. It was like having a second pair of hands. The idea of my fantasy making her own lingerie was arousing as well.

Once we had all the pieces together, we were ready for the next part.

"How do you put it together?"

"Stitching."

We used my mannequin to pull everything together. She held the pieces in place as I worked, while still wearing the soft robe. It was black and white, a simple pattern that didn't distract from her beauty.

My eyes were focused on my fingertips, watching every move I made. My fingertips were callused from years of doing this. Even if I pricked myself, I didn't bleed anymore.

Muse held the pieces together as I worked, standing directly beside me. "I like the way your face looks when you're working."

I didn't let her words interrupt me. "And how does my face look?"

"Serious. Focused. Hard."

I pulled the thread through the fabric and kept working.

"It's the same expression you wear in bed…with a few slight changes. I'd always wondered if that was the expression you wore when you were with a woman."

My hands halted once her words sank into my skin. "I used to imagine the face you made when you came. I would beat off to it in the shower. But now I know what your expression looks like…because you're the woman I take to bed every night." I started to move my hands again, and I finished the breast piece as well as the first strap.

Her cheeks were full of color.

I moved to the next strap, and she secured it in place.

"Why won't you let me sleep with you?"

My needle pierced through at the corner and then moved quickly. "I prefer to sleep alone."

"Even if you're with someone else?"

"All of my relationships are handled like business transactions. I get what I want, and then it's over. No reason for it to roll over into a new day."

"And they're just fine with that?"

"They're grateful to have any part of me at all."

She scoffed under her breath.

I stopped what I was doing and looked at her.

The corner of her mouth was raised in a smile. "Sorry… that's just the most arrogant thing I've heard you say."

I ignored her insult and returned to concentrating. "I'm sure I'll top it."

"What if I wanted to sleep with you? You know, instead of being kicked out."

"I didn't kick you out."

"You kicked me out nicely," she said. "Even though I was pretty much asleep."

"I don't like to sleep with people. I like having the bed all to myself. I like not listening to someone breathe beside me. I like to be alone. It's just how I am."

"Sounds lonely…"

"Not at all." I tightened the thread and secured the pieces together.

"And you wouldn't make an exception for me?"

"I already did," I reminded her.

"But again?"

"No. Probably not." The upper left side of the lingerie was complete. Now I needed to work on the right side.

"Does that mean you don't want to have a family someday?"

This time, I pinned the pieces against the mannequin so I wouldn't need her assistance anymore. "Why are you interrogating me?"

"I'm not. Just asking you a few questions."

"It feels like an interrogation."

"An interrogation is when someone forces you to answer questions you don't want to."

"Exactly." I pulled her hand away from the mannequin. "I can take it from here. Go sit down."

She stepped back, the hurt written on her face. "Is it that horrible that I want to know the man I'm sleeping with? I'm the closest person to you in the world. I'm your confidant, your inspiration. And I'd like to be your friend. Let me be your friend, Conway."

She continued to pull me into situations I didn't want to be in. She forced me to give up parts of myself I never thought I'd share with anyone else. And when I resisted, she somehow made me feel guilty for it. Not once in my life had I bent over backward for someone like this. She was the only woman who had this invisible power over me.

"If you don't want me to be your friend, then fine. But I need you to be mine. I'm in a different country, and I'm isolated from everyone I've ever known. I need someone to talk to. I need more than just sex…I need friendship."

"I don't have friends." I grabbed another spool of thread.

"I don't believe that."

"Have you seen me with anyone?" I challenged.

"I've heard you mention your cousin Carter a few times. And you have your family and Nicole. You have people to talk to. I only have Marco…and he doesn't really count."

My hands got back to work on the mannequin. I listened to everything she said, but I tried to tune it out. But when she had a beautiful voice like that, it was impossible for me to ignore her. When she was honest and vulnerable with me, I couldn't tune her out.

If I were going to keep her for a lifetime, I'd have to make some changes. There would never be a time when she wouldn't be around, unless I went on a business trip. So it made sense to make our relationship as positive as possible. "I'm not sure how I feel about having a family."

She was quiet for a while after I finally answered her. She sat on the stool at the table and crossed her legs, her curled hair trailing down one shoulder. "You don't want kids?"

"Sometimes I do. Sometimes I don't."

"What are your two arguments?"

I kept working while carrying on the conversation at the same time. "I had a great childhood. My parents are good people. They worked hard to raise us and maintain a close relationship with us. I like being a part of something. That's something I'd like to continue on to the next generation. But having kids is a lot of work. I'm very busy with my career, and I'm not sure if I have the time or energy to raise a family. Besides, I would need a wife. I'm not interested in having one of those right now."

"Why can't you have a family anyway?" she asked.

"I definitely need a partner," I said. "The mother of my

children would stay home and raise them so I could continue my work."

"A nanny."

"No," I said. "I don't want to pay someone to raise my kids. Defeats the purpose."

"Then why don't you go the wife route?"

I'd already explained that to her. "I can't care about someone. It'll interfere with my work."

"Really?" she asked. "Based on your designs, something must have inspired you…"

I tightened the thread and looked at her face, knowing exactly what she was talking about. I may have compromised with her in order to make our situation work, but that didn't mean anything. "Now look who's arrogant."

"I'm just saying…feeling something isn't the worst thing in the world."

"What I felt last night was passion and good sex. Nothing else." I wouldn't let her think there was more to it than that. And judging by the coldness she showed me, her attraction to me was purely physical as well.

"Good sex?" she asked with a smile. "I'm glad you enjoyed it too."

It was obvious I enjoyed it. "Just to be honest with you, you'll probably never have children." I shifted my eyes back to my hands.

"You would really take that away from me?" she asked in surprise.

"Yes." I didn't pay that kind of money to have a mom with her kids in the house. And I certainly wouldn't be the father of her children, so that would just make it more awkward.

"You'd better change your mind because I have to have children, Conway. That's a dream I've always had. The reason I went to school and worked hard to make something of myself was so I could have a family."

"Not my problem."

She narrowed her eyes fiercely. "You won't live forever, Conway. Who will inherit your legacy when you're gone?"

"Vanessa," I answered. "I'm sure she'll have children."

"But they won't be your children, Conway. And they won't be Barsettis either."

I always thought my legacy would be my lingerie. Barsetti Lingerie was immortal and would live on for hundreds of years. Maybe it would never die out. Maybe it would always be around. "But Barsetti Lingerie will continue."

"And who will run it?"

I had no idea.

She rested her arm on the table and leaned against it. She wore a confident look, like she knew she had me cornered.

My hand flinched with the needle before I kept going. "You want to have my children, Muse?"

She laughed like I'd just made a joke.

"Do you?" I pressed.

Her chuckles died away when she realized I was being serious. "I wasn't offering, if that's what you're asking. But I suppose if I'm never going to leave, at least it'll give me a way to have children. And you're a very handsome man, so I know I'd have handsome sons."

"And beautiful daughters."

She smiled and her eyes softened.

I hadn't had Muse for very long so I didn't see that far into the future, but she was my biggest inspiration. She was my ultimate fantasy. If a woman were to bear my children, who else would be better?

No one.

I finished the piece and stepped back to examine it, to see the entire image together.

She stared at it too. "I like it. But it looks complicated to get on and off."

I grabbed one of the straps and tugged on it. They were created from nylon so they stretched far and tightened back to their original elasticity. I shifted them on the mannequin, making the crotch of the figure visible.

She raised an eyebrow. "So…there're no bottoms?"

"No."

"Huh…"

"The straps can be adjusted so the tits can be exposed. That way it really moves like rope."

She continued to stare at it, the sides of her robe coming loose from her shoulder. "Not gonna lie…pretty hot."

I chuckled. "People say I'm a brilliant designer…I just know how I like to fuck women. And I'd love to fuck you wearing this."

"Then when will it be ready?"

Instantly, my cock hardened in my slacks. She used to be timid and cold, but now her eagerness was beginning to grow. Perhaps being a little nicer to her really was worth it. I thought I wanted to treat her like a prisoner, to push her down and take her whenever I wanted. But watching her want me was much more rewarding.

I tossed the thread on the table and placed the needle in my pocket. I slowly walked toward her, my shoes lightly tapping against the hardwood floor. I stopped and stared at her, looking into her bright blue eyes. My fingers went to her chin and slowly lifted her gaze, forcing her to look at me harder. I dragged the back of my forefinger down her neck and to her collarbone. "You want me, Muse?" My fingers moved farther down her stomach until I reached the sash holding her robe together. I pulled on it, making it come loose and reveal her perfect body. "You never have to ask. You can have me whenever you want."

"Right here?" she whispered. "Right now?"

I gripped the edges of her stool and leaned down, bringing my face level with hers. "Anytime."

Her fingers reached for my tie, and she slowly dragged me toward her. Her eyes were focused on my lips.

Kissing still felt wrong, like it was something I shouldn't be doing. But I enjoyed every second of it, enjoyed kissing her more than any other woman in my life. She might be inexperienced in every other way, but she certainly knew how to move her lips.

My mouth pressed against hers, and the second our lips touched, I stopped thinking about everything else. Nicole could walk in at that moment, but that wouldn't stop me. The quicker I gave my design to her, the quicker it would be produced. But now that was the last thing on my mind.

Muse was the only thing I was thinking about.

Her hands moved up my chest, and she slowly popped open my buttons. My tie was next, and soon she pushed my shirt off my body. It hit the floor quietly, and then her hands explored my bare skin.

Her nails dug into me, accompanied by her moans. She was already writhing against me, and I'd barely touched her yet. Maybe my lingerie turned her on the way it turned me on. Maybe she was jealous of the way Veronica and Juliet touched me. Maybe my focused expression turned her on.

Whatever it was, I didn't give a damn.

She got my slacks loose, and I pulled my boxers down slightly until the top of my cock emerged.

I lifted her from the stool and carried her to the bed in the corner. I used the bed for photography and so the models could be comfortable during long breaks. I never used it for sex, but now that was about to change.

The second I set her down, she yanked my slacks and boxers down to my knees.

I kicked off my shoes and crawled on top of her, my lips pressed to her mouth. "Tell me how you want me, Muse." It was the first time she'd made a move on me, the first time she'd wanted me. It was a different kind of fantasy. I enjoy watching other women want me, but to have the most gorgeous woman on the planet want me…was completely different.

"Like this…" Her hands moved up my chest, and she wrapped her arms around my neck.

My arms were pinned behind her knees, and I directed the head of my cock inside her. I felt her wetness immediately, even without extensive foreplay. I pushed inside her a little harder, feeling her body accommodate me much better than ever before.

She moaned into my mouth, her nails cutting into me.

I slid inside her the rest of the way, surrounded by her warm slickness. "Fuck…Muse." I could never get used to how incredible her pussy was. I'd spent a fortune on it, and I was definitely getting every penny's worth when I was inside her.

Her hands moved to my ass, and she pulled me inside her. "Conway…"

Jesus Christ.

Instead of fucking her slow and easy like I had before, I went hard. I rocked the bed with my quick thrusts, hitting her good and deep. Her virginity was long gone, and now I fucked her as hard as I wanted.

And she enjoyed every second of it.

Her nails moved to my back, and she scratched lines into my body. Her lips stopped moving against mine because she couldn't kiss me anymore. All she did was moan, no longer in control of her body.

Fuck, watching her enjoy me made me want to come.

"Deeper…"

I widened her legs farther and hit her balls-deep. I rocked her harder, her tits shaking up and down. My muscles tightened with my movements, my ass clenching hard. Whatever this beauty wanted, I would give it to her.

"God…yes…" Her head rolled back, and she closed her eyes.

"Look at me."

Her eyes snapped open again, and she gripped my shoulders. Her face started to change, her mouth started to open. She breathed through the thickness between her legs. She started to plummet into the climax, her mind and body combining into one. "Conway…."

Our eyes were locked together, and she was completely mine. She came around my dick, her small pussy tightening even more around me. Her nails almost drew blood, and her screams nearly pierced my eardrums.

"You're beautiful when you come." After that performance, I didn't have the endurance to keep going. I just wanted to finish, just wanted to dump all my arousal inside her. I wanted my come to sit inside her during the entire ride home. Once we were there, I would give her even more.

I grabbed the back of her neck as I finished, pumping inside her when I released. I felt my own come coat my dick, mixed with her arousal. We were combined together completely, my cock taking all of her.

She moved her fingers through my hair once we were finished, her chest flushed pink and her nipples hard. Her eyes became lidded with exhaustion, like she could fall asleep right then and there.

Thankfully, Nicole didn't walk in and see my bare ass.

I pulled out of her then pulled up my slacks.

She lay there, thoroughly fucked and beautiful.

"I have a few things to finish. I'll let you know when I'm done." I grabbed one of the blankets and pulled it over her body. That way she would be hidden from view if anyone walked in. If Nicole or one of the models knew Muse was naked, I didn't care.

She was my muse. And I enjoyed my muse.

———

I WAS SITTING at my desk in my office when Vanessa called.

"What?" I would always take her calls, but that didn't mean I wanted to talk to her.

"Why can't you just say hi? It's the same number of syllables."

Just to be an ass, I said it again. "What?"

"Don't worry, I'm not calling to talk to you. I just want Sapphire's number."

I stared straight ahead with a blank look on my face. "What?"

"Seriously, stop. You're being annoying."

"No, now I'm actually asking. Why do you want her number?"

"To talk to her…?" Vanessa's smartass attitude seemed to get worse every time I spoke to her. "Why else would I want her number?"

"But why?"

"Uh, because she's going to be my sister-in-law someday, and I'd like to get to know her."

My hand immediately tightened into a fist. The damage Muse had caused was getting worse. "I'm not going to marry her, Vanessa."

"Well, not tomorrow. But I still want to get to know her. She's really cool."

I didn't want the two of them interacting—at all. It would give Muse more power over me. And she might let something slip that would give up the whole charade. "She's busy."

"All the time?" she asked. "I can't even text her?"

There was no way around this. I'd have to cooperate, or that would be more suspicious. "She doesn't have a phone…"

"What?" she snapped. "You can't be serious."

"She dropped her old one in the toilet and never got around to replacing it."

"Aren't you a billionaire? Can't you buy the poor girl a new phone?"

I rubbed my temple, feeling the rage burn through my skin. "Yes, I'm just busy."

"Well, I'll take her to go pick up one—"

"I'll get it, Vanessa."

She finally turned quiet. "Why are you being a dick?"

"I'm not."

"Yes, you are. I'm over here trying to make an effort to make Sapphire feel welcome, and you're cockblocking me."

"I'm what?"

"You heard what I said. I just got out of class and it's hot as hell outside, so I'm coming by to use the pool. Ask Sapphire to join me."

"You're just inviting yourself over?" Man, my sister was a pain in the ass.

"You told me I'm free to come by whenever I want."

"I mean, if you're in trouble or something."

"Well, I'm in trouble right now. I'm bored and I want to hang out with your lady. Get over it."

"Vanessa—"

Click.

I almost threw the phone out the window. "Fuck." I left my desk and searched for Muse in the house. She wasn't in her bedroom, so I could only assume she was out at the stables. I walked across the grounds and found her in the barn. She was lifting bales of hay and carrying them back into the stables.

I didn't realize how strong she was.

"Muse."

She set the bale on the pile then wiped her hands on her dirty jeans. "Hey." Today, she wore a white Stetson. Now that she was getting more serious about working outside, Dante picked her up better work clothes. She had thick denim jeans, brown boots, and a collared shirt that she tied at the waist.

Sexiest fucking cowgirl I'd ever seen.

But I couldn't get distracted right now.

Not even by the small drop of sweat that was rolling down her chest toward the valley between her tits.

"My sister is being a pain in the ass right now."

"Vanessa?" Muse pulled off her hat and wiped her forehead with the back of her arm. "She seems sweet to me."

"Of course you two get along," I said sarcastically. "She's on her way here now because she wants to hang out by the pool with you. She originally asked for your phone number, but I told her you didn't have one. If she asks, you dropped your phone in the toilet, and we're getting you a new one."

Muse rested her hands on her hips and shifted her weight to one foot. "That was nice of her. When will she be here?"

"About thirty minutes."

"It's pretty hot today, so I'd love to turn in early, especially to take a swim." She started toward the house.

My arms circled her waist, and I pulled her back toward me. "Don't say a damn thing to her, alright?"

"Wasn't going to." She moved out of my embrace again.

I snatched her by the arm and pulled her back. "My sister is a lot smarter than she lets on. She poses as a fun and carefree girl, but she's analytical and observant. If you aren't careful, she might notice something. And I don't need to remind you what I'll do to you if you decide to throw me under the bus." I wouldn't be able to deal with the devastation from my family. If they knew I bought Muse like a farm animal and kept her as a pet, they'd never look at me the same. When I told them I wanted to be a lingerie designer, they never questioned me. When I was out with different women every night, they never commented on it. But this…they would have a few things to say about. I could deal with my mother's slap and my father's fist. But I couldn't deal with their disappointment.

"What will you do to me?" She tilted up her head to look into my face, her blue eyes narrowing provocatively.

"What I have to."

"Which is?" She pressed me, forcing me to say it out loud.

"I'll hurt you."

She stepped closer to me, her hand moving to my stomach. "We both know you won't. But I'll keep your secret anyway. I've been enjoying our arrangement…" Her hand slid down my stomach before she stepped away.

I turned to watch her go, my eyes examining that luscious

ass and those full hips. She had my neck under her boot, and if she wanted to cross me, it would be easy for her to do. I'd made the effort to be gentle and kind, despite how much it contradicted my nature, so it would be wrong for her to betray me.

It didn't seem like she would.

But I really had no idea. If she and Vanessa became good friends, there was no telling what might happen.

I didn't like anyone having this kind of power over me.

5

Sapphire

Vanessa swam around in the pool in her blue bikini with her hair pulled into a bun. Sunglasses were on the bridge of her nose, and the sun hit her olive skin and made it glow.

I lay in the lounge chair next to the water, my body drying off after my dip in the water. The pool overlooked the rest of the property, including the barn and stables in the distance. I could be out there working my ass off in the heat, and I was glad I was lounging by the pool today instead. I was there every single day of the week, so it was nice to do something else for a change. "How are your art classes going?"

"There are days when I love it and days when I don't love it so much." She swam to the steps of the pool and sat down so most of her body was still submerged in the water. "The days I love it are days when we're actually painting. The days I hate it are when we're learning about art history and blah, blah…" Her sunglasses covered her eyes, but it seemed like she was rolling them. "I understand why it's important to understand the various periods of art history and whatnot, but sometimes it's a real snoozefest."

I chuckled, finding Vanessa's personality refreshing. Conway and his father were both intense men, quiet and constantly brooding. They said very little with words and spoke more with their silence. His mother didn't share that level of severity, but she wasn't as blunt as her daughter. Vanessa was totally real, spitting out her honest thoughts regardless of how they made her look. She wasn't committed to being the perfect student. There were things she didn't care about, and she was upfront about it.

"Did you go to school?"

I tried not to pause for too long before I gave my response. Lying was a lot more difficult than I realized. Whatever I said to her, I would have to remember it and repeat it to the rest of his family. "I went to college for business, but I dropped out when I couldn't afford it anymore. I moved here to pursue a modeling career because it didn't cost any money."

"I heard university in America is expensive. My art school isn't cheap, but that's because it's private."

"So you want to be a professional artist?"

"I guess," she said. "There's no such thing as a professional artist. I guess I just wanted to get better at my art since I enjoy doing it. More than likely, I'll just work for the winery and do a few pieces on the side. But I wanted to try something different now rather than regret it later."

"Makes sense."

"My parents think I'm a great artist, but they're my parents…of course, they're going to say that."

"What does Conway think?"

"He says my paintings are amazing." She shook her head slightly. "But he's blind like my parents."

"Seems pretty sweet to me."

"He can be sometimes," she said. "He pretends he hates me with some of the bullshit he says, but all of his actions indicate otherwise. He's more protective of me than my own parents. It's ridiculous. Is he like that with you?"

I couldn't hold back the chuckle that launched from my throat. "Very."

"How do you stand him?" she asked seriously. "He's too much sometimes."

I knew he cared about his sister a lot. I saw it every single time he was around her. Her opinion of him meant the world to him. If it didn't, he wouldn't have compromised with me. I knew he didn't want to do it. He didn't want to treat me like a real person. He preferred to keep me as a prisoner that he could enjoy whenever he felt like it, but his sister's opinion humbled him. It forced him to be a better man. And I liked it when he was a better man. "He has a lot of good qualities…even though he doesn't show them too often."

"But he must show them to you more often than the rest of the world. Anytime I see him on TV or at work, he's like a robot. He doesn't even seem happy. He's so focused, and he looks totally miserable."

"He just concentrates really hard…" And looks incredibly sexy as he does it.

"So that's how you met? You became one of his models?"

"Yeah. I auditioned to be in his lineup, and it just took off from there…"

"When did you move in?"

I tried to keep my timetable straight. "About a month ago."

She left the steps and started to swim across the pool. She moved to the other side and leaned against the steps over there. "Does that mean you love my brother?"

This whole conversation was a lie, so it should be easy for me to spit out another one. But when I thought about the way Conway made me feel, I didn't know what to say. He was kind to me when I first met him. Sometimes he spat out rude comments here and there, but he was still good to me. He was gentle with me, even made me feel safe. If he were totally evil, he wouldn't have given me an advance in pay. He would have told me to get on my knees and work for it. And he certainly wouldn't have dropped a fortune just to save me. When I considered all of that, I knew I respected him.

Our arrangement was based on lust rather than love. But I felt something forming between us, a beautiful friendship that grew stronger with every passing day. There was trust and understanding. I stopped feeling like a prisoner and felt like a partner. I didn't know where it would lead, but I knew it would only get better as time passed. The house was beginning to feel like home, a place I never wanted to leave. If Conway let me go, I wasn't even sure what I would do with myself. Where would I go? In the end, this was the only place I really wanted to be.

He saved me.

"Of course I do." I finally forced the words out, unsure how I felt about them. It was a lie, but it didn't quite feel like one. I definitely felt a strong affection for him, respect and fondness. It wasn't romantic love, but it was something. If I were truly repulsed by him, I didn't think I could say the words out loud.

"He's so in love with you. So obvious."

This time, I stopped myself from laughing. "You think so?"

"Definitely. I've never even seen him with a woman before. You know, besides on TV for shows or whatever. He's never brought a woman to dinner. He's never even mentioned his personal life. Even when we were growing up, girls weren't around. I wondered if he was gay for a while, especially when he started to sew."

Conway was the straightest man I'd ever met. Masculine, sexual, and intense, he was the polar opposite of gay. Even with a needle and thread in his fingertips, he oozed raw sexual magnetism.

"And then we find out that Conway not only has a girlfriend, but she's living with him." Vanessa leaned back against the stairs, getting her body wet but sparing her hair. "It was all my parents and I could talk about on the drive. And my parents adore you, by the way."

"They do?" I only spent a few hours with them. That wasn't enough time for them to really form an opinion about me. Since I didn't view them as my boyfriend's parents, I hadn't been nervous at all. They were just people. Maybe that was why it was so easy for me to get along with them. And I enjoyed making Conway squirm as I pinned him underneath my thumb.

"Absolutely. My mother thinks you're the most gorgeous woman in the world, and my father thinks you'll straighten Conway out. He thinks you're turning him into a better man."

His mother thought I was gorgeous? His father thought I straightened him out? Who knew getting a man's parents to like you would be so easy? "Your parents are really nice. Conway is lucky to have such a great family."

"And a very awesome sister," she said with a smile.

"Yes," I said with a chuckle. "So, you aren't seeing that guy anymore?"

"The one I went out with one time?" she asked. "No. He asked me out in class one day, and I thought he was nice, so I said yes. But I didn't feel a connection or anything. So I just told him it wasn't going to work out. They said when you really fall in love, you know within the first twenty-four hours…and I definitely wasn't feeling it."

I thought of my first interaction with Conway. He dismissed the entire room as if he had the power of a king. He circled around me like a predator looking for a weak spot on his prey. He owned the room with his power and intensity. He made my breathing hitch, made me scared in a way that I wasn't around Knuckles. I sensed Conway's authority, and that somehow made me feel smaller. I studied his wide shoulders and chiseled forearms. I observed the facial hair that sprinkled his jaw. I noticed everything about him within a few seconds. My inexperienced body instantly hummed to life. "You'll date a lot of frogs before you find the prince."

"That's what they say," she said with a sigh. "But I'm young and I'm looking to have fun right now, not necessarily settle down. It annoys me that men are expected to settle down as late as possible, but women are expected to marry as young as possible."

"Conway did mention that."

"What did he say?" She pulled her sunglasses on top of her head so she could see me better.

"That he would be relieved if you settled down with a

powerful man. That way he wouldn't have to worry about you."

"He doesn't have to worry about me," she argued. "I'm a lot smarter than he gives me credit for."

He'd mentioned that too.

"And a woman doesn't need to stand behind a man. I'm perfectly capable of taking care of myself."

I'd thought the same thing until I got mixed up with Knuckles. Now I was completely powerless, with no control over my own destiny. The second I wasn't under Conway's protection, I would be hunted down and raped. I was grateful Conway had looked after me from the second he laid eyes on me. He wasn't a saint by any means, but I'd be worse off without him. Now I understood just how vulnerable I was. I actually needed this man…as much as I hated to admit it. "He just cares about you, Vanessa. And what woman wouldn't want to be protected by a powerful man who adores her?"

"I like the idea of being with a perfect man, but not because I need him—just because I want him." She tapped the water with both of her palms. "Now, are you going to get in? You've been lying there for like thirty minutes."

"It's nice in the sun." I raised my arms over my head and gripped the top of the chair.

"You're already so tan. How did you get that color?"

"I work in the stables every day."

Her jaw dropped. "You work out there?" She pointed to the barn. "In this heat?"

"I like taking care of the horses. Gives me something to do."

"Aren't you busy modeling?"

"Not really. I mainly help Conway with his designs now."

"Oh, that's right," she said with a nod. "I remember him saying that now…because he's an overprotective and jealous man."

"Very."

She pulled off her sunglasses and set them on the edge of the pool. "I'm going out with some friends on Saturday night. You want to come along?"

It would be nice to get out of the house and do something with someone besides Conway. He was the only person I spent time with, other than Marco and Dante. Vanessa and I got along well, so it would be nice to have another friend. "Yeah, sure. What are you guys doing?"

"Dinner, because eating is what we do best. And then we'll probably go to a club."

I suspected Conway wouldn't like that. "Sounds fun."

"Milan is such a great city. There's always stuff to do. You'll like it."

My experience with Milan up until that point hadn't been great. Maybe a night on the town would change my opinion about it. Last time I was there on my own, I was stripped naked and sold in the basement of an opera house. Hopefully, I wouldn't end up in the same place this time.

"Look who it is…" Vanessa looked past me, seeing Conway approach.

He came to my side in jeans and a black t-shirt, his body chiseled and his face handsome. He looked like a powerhouse in a suit, but when he was dressed in regular clothes, he looked just as sexy. And when he wore nothing at all, he looked the sexiest.

He stared down at me, his eyes roaming over my body in my bikini. He had no shame, not caring that his sister was close by. "Having fun?"

"We were a second ago." Vanessa had always been nice to me, but the second her brother was around, she returned to her role of being his younger sibling. "Now, there's a huge cloud over the sky."

He ignored her, keeping his eyes on me. "You look beautiful by the pool."

I stared at him through my sunglasses and felt my nipples harden against my bikini top. I'd been the recipient of that gaze enough times to know how possessive it was. If Vanessa weren't around, he'd lift up my top and suck my nipples until they were raw. He'd pull me into the pool and fuck me right against the wall. I tried to fight the heat that flushed my skin, but the burn was difficult to stave off.

I started to sweat, and that had nothing to do with the hot sun.

I had to break eye contact because it was becoming too intense—especially in front of his sister. If I could read his intentions so well, what if she could too?

"Sapphire and I are going out on Saturday night with some of my friends," Vanessa said. "Girls' night out."

That broke Conway's concentration immediately. He turned his gaze on her. "Really?"

"Yep." Vanessa grabbed one of the pool floats and glided across the water.

When Conway looked at me again, I knew exactly what he was thinking.

There was no way in hell I was going.

VANESSA LEFT after we had a late lunch.

Conway had retreated to his office after our conversation, and without even saying a word to us, it was obvious he was pissed at what Vanessa said.

It was only a matter of time before he cornered me.

I went into my bedroom and showered to rinse off the chlorine, and then I dried my hair with the fanciest blow dryer I'd ever seen. It dried my hair quickly without frying it. Everything Conway put in my room was good enough for royalty. I basically had the life of a princess.

I pulled on my underwear and then looked in my closet for something to wear. Dante was always placing new outfits in my wardrobe, usually summer dresses. Everything was designer quality, so it felt like I was going shopping every time I opened the doors. I found a white sundress with matching sandals, so I pulled that out to wear for the evening.

The door opened without warning. "If you think you're going out on Saturday, then my sister is making you as dumb as she is." He slammed the door behind him, all the veins in his forearms popping with adrenaline. Even the vein in his neck was vibrating.

"What did we say about knocking?" I set the dress on the bed and returned the hanger to the closet.

"Not in the mood." His jaw was harder than I'd ever seen it.

"You don't say…" I knew he was truly pissed when he saw me stand in my thong and bra and did nothing about it. I pulled the white dress over my head and felt it fall to my knees. It was longer in the back, hitting the floor slightly.

He marched to me and got in my face, intimidating me with his towering height. "You aren't going."

"So, you suggest I stay locked up all the time?" I asked incredulously. "For the rest of my life?"

"No. You can go out, just not on a Saturday night with a

bunch of pretty women in a dangerous city. Have them come over here."

"No one is going to want to do that."

"Why don't you just ask?"

"I'm not changing the plans," I snapped. "Conway, I can't blow off your sister. She asked me to do something, and I want to go. I need more in my life than staying here all the time and working. Vanessa knows the city. I'm sure she knows to avoid the bad part of town."

Now his eyes burned as they looked at me. "Vanessa is a fucking idiot. I don't want her going out either."

"There's no other way around this. I'm going."

"You do what I say—and you aren't going."

I crossed my arms over my chest. "What did we talk about?"

"This is different. I'm overriding you."

"No, we can compromise on this like two adults. That's how this works, remember?"

He inched closer to me, his face nearly touching mine. "We can compromise on a lot of things, but not this. This is about safety. I'm not letting you run around in Milan with a bunch of stupid women who think they're untouchable. Of all people, you should understand why I'm not allowing you to leave."

"Exactly," I said. "And I still want to go. I don't want to be afraid of the world, Conway. I'm not going to be sleeping by a dumpster this time."

He somehow clenched his jaw tighter. "The answer is no."

"I'm not asking for your permission."

His hand shot out, and he gripped my neck.

I didn't flinch, knowing he wouldn't actually hurt me.

"You don't even have the right to ask for permission—because I own you."

My eyes shifted back and forth as I looked into his gaze. He was so close I could barely see his features. All I could feel was his anger as it swept over me. I knew his behavior didn't stem from psychotic possessiveness, but terror. "Conway, there's no possible explanation I could give to Vanessa without making it obvious."

"Tell her you're busy."

"And the next time she asks?" I kept my voice steady even though I was the one being held by the throat.

"Same thing."

"That's not going to work, and you know it." I wrapped my fingers around his wrist. "I'm going, Conway. You can grab me by the neck all you want, but it's not going to change anything. I'll be careful."

"You've never been careful."

"And that's why I'll be careful now." I pushed his hand down.

He released me.

"I like your sister. She's the only friend I have."

"You don't need friends. You have me."

A soft smile crept onto my lips. "You're my friend, huh?"

"Isn't that what you wanted?" he whispered.

"It is. So, why don't you come with me?"

He tilted his head slightly, the anger slowly fading away. "I thought this was a girls' thing."

"It is. And I'm going. So if you're really that worried about me, then you can come along. Or you can just get over it. But that's your decision. All I know is, I'm going." I moved into him and pressed my lips against his. I gave him a soft kiss, one that immediately made him close his eyes and respond to me. Then I stepped away, noticing the way his body went soft. "The decision is yours."

DANTE GOT me a silver dress that reached slightly past my thighs. It was skintight, short, and had small straps over the shoulders. A matching pair of silver heels went with it. I looked at myself in the mirror and fixed my lipstick before I walked downstairs.

Conway was in the entryway in dark jeans and a collared shirt. He watched me walk down the stairs with a dark expression, his eyes smoldering the closer I came to him. He was both annoyed and pleased by my outfit.

I had a black clutch with money and my phone tucked inside. I finally had my own phone, but unfortunately, I didn't have anyone to call. I stopped in front of him, watching him look me over. "I'm ready."

"Where are the rest of your clothes?" He raked his eyes across my body.

"That's saying something coming from a lingerie designer." I flipped my hair and walked past him.

He slapped his hand against my ass then snatched me, yanking me against his chest as he dug his hand into my hair. He immediately moved in for a kiss.

It was the first time I denied him. "No."

"No?" His eyes narrowed in surprise since he never heard that word.

"Later."

"Later?" he asked incredulously.

"Yes. Later." I pulled my arm out of his grasp. "I want you to stare at me all night until you can't stand it anymore. Then when we get home, I'll reward you for your good behavior…if you can manage it."

All I got in return was a quiet groan. But when there was no argument, I knew he was cooperating. We got inside his blacked-out SUV and hit the road.

I pulled out my phone and saw a message from Vanessa.

We're heading to Club Bellissima. Do you know how to get there?

I typed back. *Yeah, I'm sure I can find it.*

Great! See you soon. I put my phone back in my clutch.

"What did she say?" He drove with one hand and kept his eyes on the road. It was eight in the evening, so we would be there by nine.

"They're at Club Bellissima."

"You're kidding."

"No. Why?"

He shook his head slightly. "No reason."

We drove the rest of the way in silence. Conway didn't hide his underlying annoyance. He was still pissed about this excursion altogether. But this was the only compromise we could reach. I was going out whether he liked it or not. His only option was to come with me.

We arrived in Milan forty minutes later and parked in a lot behind a building. There were no other cars there.

"Where are we?"

"I own this building."

"Oh…" I looked around the empty parking lot. It looked like an apartment complex, but no one else seemed to live there.

"This is where I stay when I'm in Milan. I bought the building because I don't like neighbors."

"An expensive solution. How far away is the club?"

"Just around the block."

We got out of the car then walked toward the sidewalk. My heels were five inches tall, so I couldn't keep up with the stride of a six-foot-three man. Thankfully, Conway slowed his pace so I wouldn't have to work so hard to keep up.

He didn't hold my hand.

Not that I expected him to.

We arrived at the club and saw the line down the sidewalk and all the way around the building.

"Popular place, huh?" I asked.

"A bit." Conway walked past the end of the line and moved to the front.

I trailed behind him. "What are you doing?"

"Getting inside."

"Line is back there, Conway."

"Not for me." He reached the front of the line where the four bouncers were. All they did was look at him before they opened the door and allowed him inside.

They didn't exchange a single word.

I followed behind him and entered the dark club. There were several bars positioned throughout the two floors, and all the booths were made of dark blue leather with black tables. Pretty women were everywhere, and all the men were staring at them. Music blared from the speakers, and we were surrounded by the loud volume of shouted conversations.

Conway parted the crowd everywhere he went, either because people were intimidated or because they recognized his face. He didn't hold my hand or pull me close to him, hardly touching me at all.

It seemed like he was doing it on purpose.

I looked up to the second floor and saw Vanessa sitting with two other women. "I see them."

"Alright. I'll be over here."

"You won't be joining us?" I asked.

"Don't worry, I'll keep an eye on you." He slid one hand into his pocket and walked away, heading to the bar.

I didn't want him there to begin with, so that worked out in my favor. I took the stairs to the second floor and spotted the girls chatting away, their drinks sitting in front of them. One was blond, another was brunette. Vanessa had dark hair like mine, nearly black.

Vanessa was in a tight black dress, her hair curled and pulled over one shoulder. She had toned arms and rounded shoulders. A gold necklace hung around her throat.

"Sorry I'm late." I sat at the end of the curved leather booth.

"Hey!" Vanessa smiled then grabbed my wrist. "You look so hot. These are some of my friends." She introduced us, and we got to talking. "Sapphire is dating my brother. Well, not dating. She's living with him."

"Conway?" Stephanie, the blonde, asked.

"Yep," Vanessa said. "And she's got him wrapped around her finger."

Couldn't be further from the truth, but I smiled anyway. "He's a good man. I know I'm lucky."

Laura, the brunette, took a long drink of her cosmo. "I've been in love with him for years."

"Everyone has been in love with him for years," Stephanie said. "Including me."

Vanessa made a face. "He's not everything he's cracked up to be."

"What are you talking about?" Laura said. "He's loaded and sexy. He's the perfect man."

I wasn't jealous that her friends thought Conway was attractive, but I didn't like the way he was objectified. There was more to him than being rich and hot. "He's also very generous and compassionate. He takes care of his models, and he's good to the people who work for him. He's also a good friend…"

Vanessa grinned. "Head over heels…"

I wanted to contradict her, but I knew I shouldn't.

A man appeared at the table holding a vodka cranberry. He set it down in front of me, wearing a grin on his face.

He wasn't the bartender I ordered from, and that wasn't even the drink I ordered. "Uh, I think you got my order mixed up with someone else's."

He slid into the booth beside me, making himself comfortable.

I immediately shifted away, my personal space in jeopardy. After what I experienced, I didn't like it when anyone got too close to me. It immediately set off radars in my head.

"I'll get you whatever you want, sweetheart." He draped his arm over the back of the chair. "Cosmo?"

I scooted farther away from him. "How about you just take your drink back and learn how to not be creepy?"

"Yeah, you're so creepy." Vanessa snapped her fingers and pointed to the other side of the room. "Now, go be creepy elsewhere."

Just as he leaned forward to say something to her, he was yanked out of the booth and onto the floor.

Conway kicked him to the side then pressed his foot against his chest, applying pressure right against his lungs. Despite the violence of the situation, the bouncers watched from the first floor with their arms crossed over their chests, staying out of it even though it was their job to interfere. "Get the fuck out." Conway stepped back and watched the man lying on the floor.

The guy quickly got up, avoided eye contact, and bolted for the stairs.

Conway straightened the front of his shirt then slid his hands into his pockets, resuming his suave casualness before he turned his gaze on me. Obviously bubbling with irritation and rage, he looked at me like I was the one who'd done something wrong. "I can't leave you alone even for five minutes."

Stephanie and Laura both stared at Conway like he was a big piece of man meat, especially after that heroic performance he'd just given.

Vanessa wore an angry expression similar to Conway's, their sibling DNA even more apparent when they were both ticked. "What the hell are you doing here, Con?"

He slid into the booth beside me and draped his arm over my shoulders. Unlike the guy before him, his touch was sexy and welcomed. His cologne entered my nose, and his protection wrapped around me like an invisible wall. It was nothing like the creepiness that surrounded the man before him. He pulled my hair off my shoulder to expose my neck and placed a soft kiss against my pulse.

Vanessa narrowed her eyes further. "You going to answer me?"

"Do I ever answer you?" he asked coolly. He scanned the bar then raised his hand slightly, getting the attention of someone we couldn't see.

A woman appeared out of nowhere, in a skintight dress with a tray tucked under her arm. "What can I get you, sir?"

"Scotch," he answered. "My girl will have the same—on the rocks."

My girl.

I shouldn't feel warm inside, but I did.

The waitress disappeared, and Conway returned to scanning the room. The music still played overhead, and people danced in the center of the platform on the second landing. The lights were low and in hues of blue. Everything there had a blue cast to it.

"Does that mean you're staying?" Vanessa asked. "Because this is a chick thing."

Conway ignored her.

"Are you a chick?" Vanessa asked.

Conway finally turned back to her. "Pretend I'm not here. I pretend you don't exist all the time."

Vanessa narrowed her eyes. "If Sapphire weren't my friend, I'd kick you under the table."

"And I'd kick you back," Conway said. "Hard."

Vanessa took a drink, the irritation still in her eyes.

"He wouldn't let me come without him in tow," I said apologetically. "Believe me, I tried."

Conway turned away again, entertaining himself by watching the crowd. The waitress brought his drinks instantly, and he left a hundred euros on the table as a tip.

"I know," Vanessa said. "This guy follows me around when I'm on a date, so trust me, I understand."

"Aww, he's just trying to protect you," Stephanie said. "I think it's sweet."

My spine suddenly tightened in annoyance. The girls had been forthcoming about their attraction to him, and I'd let it slide because it would be impossible for any woman not to be attracted to him. But now, it kept going…and I didn't care for it.

"I think it's creepier than that guy who was just here," Vanessa said. "I'm twenty-one years old. I don't need a babysitter."

Conway remained quiet, doing his best to blend into the background and go unnoticed.

The subject changed, and we talked about one of Vanessa's art classes. The girls went to school with her, so that's where they met. They were all aspiring artists, and it reminded me of my college years. I met a lot of people who were trying to find their way in the world. Even in a different discipline, that feeling was the same.

"Ooh…" Vanessa nodded to another booth in the corner. "Check out that guy in the leather jacket."

We all turned to look. In tight jeans with dark hair and a muscular build, a guy approached the booth with a few buddies. They were all drinking beer. The guy Vanessa noticed had stubble across his face and dark eyes. He was definitely a looker, but I wouldn't have noticed him if she hadn't pointed him out.

"Damn, look at that tight ass," Stephanie said.

"Ooh, his friend is cute too," Laura said.

He reminded me of Conway in many ways, but a watered-down version. "Yeah, he's cute."

Conway turned his gaze on me—and he was pissed.

I felt the ferocity in his look. It was ice-cold and burning with a raging fire at the same time, and he looked like he might strangle me. If we were alone, he probably would have a few words to add to that look.

"Are you going to talk to him?" Laura asked.

"Definitely." Vanessa fixed her hair and then checked her lipstick with her compact.

Conway let out a quiet sigh, one packed with irritation.

"Wish me luck." Vanessa pressed her lips together to get her lipstick just right. Then she started to slide out of the booth.

"You don't just hit on some random dude in a bar." Conway was supposed to be staying quiet, but he obviously couldn't keep his promise when his sister was trying to get some action.

"And where would you like me to do it?" she asked. "In a convent?"

I did my best to hide the smirk from my face.

"You have no idea who this guy is," Conway snapped. "He could be a rapist or something."

"You think a fine-ass man like that needs to rape people to get laid?" Vanessa snapped. "You're ridiculous, Conway."

"Vanessa—"

I gripped his forearm. "Let it go, Conway."

Vanessa slid out of the booth and strutted toward the man she had her eyes set on.

Conway watched them like a hawk, his chest rising and falling slowly with barely restrained rage. "She's so fucking stupid."

"She's a single woman looking for action," I said. "Nothing wrong with that."

"There's everything wrong with it," he snapped. "She shouldn't be acting this way."

"So it's okay for you to do it but not her? I didn't realize you were so sexist."

"I'm not sexist." He kept his voice low so we couldn't be overheard. "My whole business is based on women walking around half naked. Obviously, I'm not sexist. The person I depend on most is a woman. I just don't like this…"

"You have to let it go, Conway. She's a grown woman."

"I just…" He watched Vanessa get the man's attention and start a conversation. The guy smiled down at her while holding his beer. She must have said something funny because he responded with a chuckle. "I don't want anyone to hurt her."

"Everyone gets their heart broken. It's how life is."

"That's not what I mean."

"Not every man is evil, Conway. There are men out there like Knuckles and the Skull Kings, but there are good men out there too."

"All men are evil," he said quietly. "Just in different degrees."

"Your father doesn't seem evil."

Conway turned away, obviously not wanting to open that subject.

Vanessa continued her conversation with the guy, and they seemed to be hitting it off. When he wasn't laughing, he was smiling down at her. His eyes held the same excitement, like he was genuinely interested in their conversation.

How could he not be? Vanessa looked more like a model than I did.

A man appeared at Conway's side and placed his hand on his shoulder.

I knew only someone close to him would touch him like that, unless they wanted their skull to be crushed under his boot.

The man looked to be in his fifties, and he smiled down at Conway with affection. There were obvious similarities between them, from the color of their hair and eyes to the features of their faces.

They were definitely related.

Once Conway recognized him, the tension in his shoulders died away. "Uncle." Conway slid out of the booth and straightened to his full height. He was the same size as his uncle, tall with a lean and toned appearance. "How are you?"

"You look like you're having a good time." He glanced at me before he winked at Conway.

I slid out of the booth next and extended my hand. "Pleasure to meet you. I'm—"

"I know who you are, sweetheart." He leaned in and kissed me on the cheek, disregarding my hand.

I hated the word sweetheart, but when Conway's father or uncle said it, it didn't seem so bad. It seemed affectionate and respectful. Knuckles's hold over the name had begun to fade away. "You do?"

"My brother and sister said good things." His gaze shifted back to Conway. "I heard you've been straightening him out."

"He's already pretty straight," I said with a laugh. "Never needed my help with that."

His uncle grinned. "I like you."

My cheeks blushed as I smiled. "Thanks…"

"I'm Cane," he said.

"Sapphire." He said he already knew who I was so I didn't need to introduce myself, but I did anyway.

"My uncle owns this club," Conway said. "That's why I found it ironic you girls wanted to come here."

"It's nice," I said. "Drinks are strong."

"They're only strong for pretty girls." He glanced at Vanessa, who was still talking to that guy. "Who's she talking to?"

Conway glanced over his shoulder and sighed. "She thought he was cute…"

"Should I throw him out?" Cane asked, dead serious.

Were all the Barsetti men like this? "Leave her alone. She's a grown woman. Even if she makes a mistake, good for her. If we don't make mistakes, then we'll never learn."

"There are some mistakes that shouldn't be made," Conway said darkly. "I'll keep an eye on her."

The fact that his uncle found that response normal was surprising. No wonder why Vanessa was the ornery, free-spirited woman she was. She must feel suffocated with all these overprotective men.

"I'll see you later." Cane pulled him into a hug and patted him on the back. "You look good, by the way."

Conway smiled. "Thanks. You do too."

"Obviously." He smirked. "But you only look good because of the woman on your arm."

LAURA AND STEPHANIE settled into a different table with a pair of brothers. They enjoyed their drinks and the good conversation. Vanessa hadn't stopped talking to the man she set her eyes on. Now they were alone in a booth together, talking quietly while his arm rested over the back of the leather seat. They were very close together, close enough for a kiss if the moment was right.

Conway didn't stare at them, but it was obvious he was aware of them. We could leave at any time now that the girls had broken off into different groups. There was no reason for us to stick around.

But Conway kept ordering more rounds.

And that man could drink.

He rested his fingertips around the glass while his arm remained draped over my shoulders.

"So, are we going to stay here all night and spy?"

"I'm just enjoying my drink."

"That's your fifth scotch. Looks like I'll have to drive home."

"I can drive."

"Not so sure about that…"

"Do I seem drunk?" He looked down into my face, his handsome smolder sexy.

"No."

"Then it'll be fine."

I pressed my fingertips to his chin and gently felt the beard along his jaw. The stubble was thick and coarse and scratched against my soft fingertips. I followed the outline of his jaw to his cheek. My eyes focused on his full lips, examining the man in front of me like he was a statue of the most revered king in history.

"You can have me whenever you want me, Muse."

My eyes flicked back up to his. "What makes you think I want you?"

His fingers wrapped around my slender wrist and squeezed. "I know you better than you think. I know that look in your eyes…it's the look you give when you want me to kiss you."

My legs were crossed under the table, and I felt my thighs squeeze together involuntarily. I'd seen most of the women inside that club stare at Conway at least once. He was the most eligible bachelor in Italy, and I knew women weren't just staring because of his fame. They were staring because he was more beautiful than the models he employed. It made me possessive, but it also made me feel lucky. I was the one sitting with him in that booth—not them. "Are you going to kiss me, then?"

"Not in a room full of people."

"Ashamed of me, huh?" I whispered, knowing that couldn't be true.

"I just don't want men to get off to it."

"Honestly, I think the women are more likely to get off to it…"

He rubbed his nose against mine. "You're a very jealous woman."

"No, I'm not."

His eyes narrowed as he challenged me.

"And you're one to talk."

"I'm not jealous. I'm just very possessive of my things."

"That's the exact definition of jealousy…"

"No, you're thinking of greed. I'm very greedy. I have something that I don't want anyone else to have. It's not because I care for it. It's simply because I like having something that others don't."

"That's not greedy. That's just being an asshole."

The corner of his mouth rose in a smile. "I am an asshole."

My hand moved to his thigh under the table. I slowly inched toward his waist until I felt the bulge in his jeans. His long cock was perfectly outlined, and he didn't flinch in shame for having a hard-on in the middle of a club.

My fingertips slid over his thickness and moved to the base.

He kept his eyes on me, watching me feel him up under the table. "Maybe you should wait until we get home."

"Maybe you should kiss me."

His hand cupped the back of my head, and his fingers touched my hair. "Why do you want me to kiss you so bad, Muse?"

"Why *don't* you want to kiss me? You say I'm the most beautiful woman in the world, right?"

He tucked a few strands of hair behind my ear, his eyes focusing on my lips. "Yes."

"Then prove it."

"I think I am proving it." He grabbed my hand and pressed it against his hard-on through his jeans. "Immensely."

My hand glided up his chest, and I leaned in to press my lips against his. He didn't resist me, and his eyes became lidded. But I planted a kiss on his jaw instead, trailing kisses all the way to his neck. My hand explored his chest as my plump lips devoured him, treasuring his body with my wet tongue. My mouth migrated to his ear, and I breathed into his canal. "Kiss me, Conway. Don't make me ask you again."

This time, he gripped the back of my hair and yanked on it so he could kiss me the way he wanted—deep, hard, and rough. His lips nearly bruised mine as he devoured me, crushed me against him. The beginning was intense, but then his kiss turned soft. Just as it was when we were in bed together, it was gentle and purposeful, with him feeling my lips rather than crushing them. His fingertips stopped yanking on my hair and started to caress the strands.

I wanted to undress him then and there and have him, take him deep inside me. In the beginning, I saw him as a cruel captor who treated me like a prisoner. But now I found myself wanting him as much as he wanted me. I wanted his attention, his affection. I wanted him to make me feel good just as he did before.

He moaned into my mouth, the vibration evident against my tongue. The music was too loud overhead for us to hear each other, but I could feel his intensity through his touch. The heat cranked higher and higher, and his cock was about to burst through his jeans.

He suddenly ended the kiss and turned his face away.

My nails dug into his shirt in response, unsatisfied that the kiss was over.

His jaw was clenched hard.

"Let's go home."

He glanced at Vanessa and her date.

"She's a grown woman, Conway. You need to let it go." I slid out of the other side of the booth without waiting for him. I rose to a stand, my heels sky-high and painful.

He looked me up and down, his mind switching to sex once more.

"Well, I'm leaving. Good night." I turned around and walked away, knowing he would stare at my ass the entire time.

And as I expected, he appeared behind me an instant later. His arm circled my waist, and he walked me out of the club, parting the crowd with his distinctiveness. Once we were outside, the cool air was a nice change compared to the room stifling with body heat. The breeze immediately licked the sweat off my skin.

His arm pulled me in tighter as we walked down the sidewalk together in the darkness. I used to walk down these sidewalks all the time when I picked up food or did my laundry. I used to head back to my hotel and watch TV every night because I had nothing else to do. But now my life was completely different.

We entered the building he owned and stepped inside the large garage with the single car. But he didn't walk to the blacked-out SUV. Instead, he headed to the elevator and pressed the button with his forefinger.

"Where we are going?"

All he did was stare.

The doors opened and we stepped inside. He hit the button for the top floor, and the door closed.

"If your place is on the top—"

He pressed me against the wall of the elevator and kissed me the way he had at the leather booth. But this time, it was harder—fiercer. He gripped my hips and pressed his chest against my tits. His mouth moved to my jawline and neck, and he yanked up my dress to reveal my black thong underneath. My leg was pulled around his waist, and he ground against me, pressing his hard-on right against my clit.

Felt so damn good.

"Conway…" My head rolled back as I let him kiss my neck. I felt the wonderful friction between my legs, the strength of his raging hard-on. His girth felt so good, so deep and thick. I ground back against him and dug my nails into his shoulders.

Why the fuck was this elevator moving so slow?

The elevator finally stopped and the doors opened.

Instead of waiting for me to walk, he lifted me into his arms and carried me into the apartment. He dropped me on the couch with a deep thud and then yanked my panties over my heels.

Before I could reach for his jeans, they were already off and pushed to his thighs.

"Conway." I grabbed his hips and pulled him against me.

He guided the head of his cock into my entrance then shoved himself inside me.

It always hurt slightly, but the pleasure far outweighed the discomfort. I dug my nails into his ass and pulled him into me, taking in every inch until I felt his cock bump into my cervix.

He pressed my leg against the back of the couch and pinned me into the corner. His hand moved to the back of my neck, and he gripped me as he thrust inside me. His balls smacked into my ass as he moved, tapping me over and over again.

It was exactly what I wanted, to feel this strong man on top of me. My hands moved underneath his shirt and felt the rippling muscles of his physique. All the women had stared at him with lust in their eyes, but I was the woman who went home with him—every night.

His eyes locked on to mine as he folded me underneath him. He rammed me hard, hitting me good and deep. Sweat collected on his body almost instantly, and I could feel his wildly beating heart under my palm.

"Yes…like that."

He kept up the fast pace and pressed me deeper into the fabric of his couch. I was folded and bent in different ways because he did whatever was necessary to get as close to me as possible.

He pressed his forehead to mine then kissed me—kissed me good.

That's when my pussy tightened around his length and I came all over him. "Conway…" My hand moved into the back of his hair, and I moaned against his mouth, writhing and slipping into euphoria.

He rested his forehead against mine and gave his final thrusts, his cock thickening a little more just before release.

Now I lived for his orgasms, I lived for his come. "Give me all of it…"

He moaned against my lips just as he released. He gripped my lower back and pulled me tighter against him, getting his cock as deep inside as possible. He filled me with everything he had, mounds of come that felt warm and heavy. "Like that?"

"Yes…" My legs were wide apart to accommodate him, and my hands sank to his ass again. My nails cut into his skin because I couldn't relax my knuckles. I loved the satisfied look in his eyes, the fact that he was pleased with the experience as well as his performance.

"You love my come?"

My fingertips felt his stubble. "Deeply."

He rubbed his nose against mine as he kept his dick inside me. He was soft now, but within a few minutes, he would be ready to go again. "More?"

"Please."

He growled against my mouth. "Muse…"

ONCE THE FUCKING was finally finished, he retrieved two glasses of water from the kitchen.

I pulled my dress down but let my panties stay on the coffee table as I walked to the floor-to-ceiling window. The lights from the city glowed brightly, and it seemed like the world was at his feet. His building was slightly higher than the others, so it was easy to see the beautiful cathedrals.

He handed me a glass of water.

"Thank you." I watched him as I drank, seeing the satisfied and tired expression in his eyes.

He drank his and stayed beside me, standing in just his black boxers.

"I like your place."

"Thanks."

"I haven't seen much of it, but I like what I see." It had an open kitchen and an enormous living room. He had a picturesque view on three sides of the building.

"The rest of the rooms are just bedrooms and my office."

"What about the other floors?"

"One is a personal gym."

"An entire floor?" I asked incredulously.

"Yes."

"And the others?"

He shrugged. "I didn't do anything to them. They're just empty apartments now."

"Wow…"

"I'm a very private person."

"You don't say," I said with a chuckle.

He drank the rest of his glass, his throat shifting as he downed the water. When he finished, he wiped his mouth with the back of his forearm. Even regular activities were sexy on a man like him. "We should get going."

"Why don't we just sleep here tonight?"

He set his empty glass on the table and grabbed his shirt from the floor. "I prefer Verona."

"Then why do you have this place?"

"It's closer to the office. When it snows, it's easier just to come here."

"Is there a lot of snow in the winter?"

"There can be." He buttoned his shirt and then pulled on his jeans. He pulled his phone out of his pocket and checked the screen. "Last year, we had a pretty harsh winter."

"What does Marco do in the stables then?"

"Keeps the horses warm by bringing them into the barn."

I'd never worked in the snow before. I'd have to get some new gear.

He returned his phone to his pocket and grabbed my thong from the table. "You want me to hold on to this for you?" He wrapped it around his fingers and rubbed it between his fingertips.

My panties looked a lot better on him than they did on me. I set my glass down and pulled them from his hand. "How about we just stay here? This view is so gorgeous. You can see the whole city."

His playfulness immediately evaporated. "I said we're going back to Verona. This isn't a discussion."

And just like that, the connection between us was severed. Anytime I thought we were getting closer together, something came between us and he laid down the law. He reminded me what the relationship really was. He was the owner.

I was the property.

End of story.

I didn't hold back my look of disappointment.

And Conway didn't give a damn.

He pulled on his shoes, and we left the apartment. My pussy was still full of his come, but now it didn't feel so sexy. I suddenly felt more naked than I had before. It seemed like our passionate evening together meant nothing.

Why did I ever think it meant anything?

We returned to the garage and got into the SUV. Then

Conway pulled on to the road and left Milan. The city disappeared behind us as we headed into the countryside. The farther we went, the darker the world became. Only the lights from villas and mansions could be seen from the road.

I pulled my knees to my chest and stared out the window, doing my best to cut him out of my peripheral vision.

Conway was quiet for most of the drive. "I didn't mean to anger you."

"You didn't."

"Seems that way." His baritone was deeper when he spoke more quietly. Somehow, he seemed to say more when he said less. He had the sexiest voice I'd ever heard. Even if I didn't know what his face looked like, that voice would turn me on by itself.

"I'm disappointed in you."

"Because I wanted to go to Verona?" he asked incredulously. "Verona is a lot safer than Milan. I shouldn't even have to explain myself, Muse. When I say something, you just need to listen."

"If I were just some random woman you'd picked up, you would have listened."

"What makes you think that?" he asked. "I told you women don't sleep over, so that doesn't make sense."

"But you still wouldn't speak to her that way."

"You give me too much credit," he whispered. "You think I'm only an ass to you. Trust me, I'm an ass to everyone."

"Then you should be ashamed of that."

"It's who I am. And I'm not ashamed of who I am."

I concentrated my gaze out the window even harder.

"You need to stop expecting me to treat you differently," he said. "I'm not going to. That's how it is."

"Yeah…I'm realizing that."

Conway didn't say anything else, and we were quiet for the rest of the drive. We left the car in the roundabout then walked inside the house. I didn't wait around for him, and I went straight to bed. I took off my heels and climbed to the third floor quickly, shutting the door behind me once I was in my bedroom.

When I was finally alone, I released the breath I was holding.

I didn't understand why I was so upset with him. He didn't want me to go out alone, and when some guy made a pass at me, he flipped out and made a scene about it. But he refused to give me any kind of special treatment. The second things didn't go his way, he reminded me I had no voice.

It was infuriating.

Maybe he was right when he said he was just greedy and not jealous. Maybe he really was just an ass. Maybe I wanted to see the good in him because I knew he wasn't evil. But just because he wasn't evil didn't mean he was good.

I didn't even wash my face before bed. I just pulled on a t-shirt and changed my panties before I got under the covers. The lamp was turned off, and I was swallowed by the darkness. I cleared my thoughts and stopped thinking about Conway and the night I had.

When he touched me in that booth, I felt like the only woman that mattered. When he kissed me so passionately, it seemed like I was more than just some woman. He was possessive, and he never stopped wanting me. I didn't even see him look at another woman—and beautiful women were everywhere.

But maybe none of that meant anything.

Maybe I didn't mean anything.

I TOSSED and turned in bed, sweat covering my neck and back. My lips quivered with silent screams that couldn't escape my throat. I tossed and turned constantly, shifting from left to right and twisting the sheets around my body.

It was a nightmare.

The worst one I'd ever had.

I'd just left the bar where I worked and was headed down the sidewalk. My purse was over my shoulder, and my heart was racing because I knew what was about to happen before it even happened.

I stopped in front of a pitch-black alleyway, knowing exactly what lurked in the shadows.

I should just walk away, but I didn't.

Then I heard the guttural sound of a man dying. Deadly moans escaped his lips every time a boot was kicked into his side. He was being beaten to death in the darkness, his moans growing louder until they stopped.

I was relieved they stopped, but I also knew what that meant.

Nathan was dead.

Knuckles stepped out of the blanket of shadows, his tattoos covering his body and his blue eyes piercing. He circled me like a shark, owning the sidewalk since there was no other pedestrian in sight.

He owned this city—so it was just the two of us.

I couldn't run.

Blood was on his forearms and knuckles, my brother's blood. He continued to circle, his smile wide and malicious. He lifted a forefinger and dragged it across my cheek, smearing blood across my skin. "I'm going to fuck you, sweetheart. And after you're dead, I'll fuck you again."

I bolted upright in bed, clutching my chest in desperation of trying to breathe. Sweat was stuck against the sheets, making them damp and sticky. My heart was beating so hard it hurt in my chest. I kicked the blankets off because I didn't want anything touching me.

I didn't want to be in that bed anymore.

I needed fresh air. I needed the sky. I needed somewhere that could make me feel free.

The first place I wanted to run was Conway's bedroom. There was no place in the world I felt safer than in his arms. But that idea immediately disappeared when I realized it wasn't an option.

Conway didn't care if I had a nightmare.

I pulled on jeans and a t-shirt and headed to the first floor. The house was silent, pitch black and lonely. The sweat from my body stuck to my clothes, and I could feel it drip down my back. My heart was still racing even though I knew it was just a dream. But that dream felt more real than my reality. The only place I found peace was at the stables with the horses. When I was there, I didn't have to think. I just worked until I was dead tired.

That was the only thing that could get me through this.

6

Conway

THE ALARM FROM MY PHONE SHRIEKED AT TOP VOLUME.

It wasn't the same alarm I used to wake up in the morning.

It was the alarm I used when shit got serious.

It meant a door had been opened without the code or a window had been smashed. It meant someone was trying to fuck with me—and they would regret it. I hopped out of bed and pulled on sweatpants and a t-shirt at lightning speed. Then I grabbed my semiautomatic from underneath my bed, which was fully loaded.

Dante would have heard the alarm too, and he would be appropriately armed.

The first place I went was Sapphire's bedroom. I had to make sure she was alright before I explored the rest of the house. I opened the door without knocking and saw the bedside lamp was turned on. The sheets were kicked back, and she was nowhere in sight. "Muse?" I checked the bathroom and the living room. "Muse?"

She wasn't there.

Fuck.

Now I was terrified in a whole new way.

I headed back into the hallway and took the stairs. I had my gun at the ready, prepared to kill anyone inside my house that shouldn't be there. I wanted to call out for Dante or Muse, but it was too dangerous.

"Sir?" Dante stepped into my sight at the bottom of the stairs. He held a shotgun with a bulletproof vest strapped over his chest. He wasn't just a chef and the caretaker of the house, but a man prepared to murder anyone who stepped foot inside the place without being invited. "It's Sapphire."

I stopped at the second landing. "What? Is she alright? Where is she?"

"She tripped the alarm when she left out the back door. The light from the stables in on, so she must be down there."

What the fuck was she doing down there? "It's three in the morning."

"I realize that, sir."

"What could be so important for her to go down there in the middle of the night?"

Dante lowered his gun and shrugged. "No idea, sir. Would you like me to fetch her?"

I turned the safety on my gun and set it on the ground. "No. I'll handle her." I made it to the bottom of the stairs, ferocity circling in my veins. How could she be so stupid? In her defense, I never told her about the alarm system, but she was stupid to run off in the middle of the night.

Dante pulled out a pistol from his back pocket. "Just in case?"

I wasn't walking up to Muse with a gun. I didn't have a clue what she was doing at the stables, but scaring her wasn't the best way to handle it. "No." I left out the back door she used and crossed the grass to get there quicker.

All the lights from the stables were on, and the bugs were attracted to the bright lights that highlighted the grass around the area. I entered the stables and found her leaning over the fence where one of the tamest mares was housed. Her chin was propped in her hand, and she petted the horse as it stood over her. The rest of the horses stuck their heads out, confused that there was a visitor in the middle of the night. Even Carbine was looking at her.

"What the fuck are you doing?"

She jumped two inches off the ground and even spooked the horse with her movements. "Jesus…you scared me."

"I scared you?" I snapped. "Your little stunt set off the alarm in the house. Dante and I were both armed and ready for war. What the hell were you thinking?" I came closer to her, feeling my arms shake in annoyance. "If you couldn't sleep, you could have turned on the damn TV or made a snack in the kitchen." When I was just a foot away, that's when I noticed the puffiness of her eyes. Covered with moisture and red, her eyes showed the classic signs of crying. I shut my mouth when I realized this was more complicated than just not being able to sleep.

She quickly turned away, hiding her face from me. "I'm sorry…I didn't know about the alarm. If I'd known, I wouldn't have left." She trailed her fingers up and down the snout of the horse, petting the mare gently.

I came up beside her, feeling like an ass when I shouldn't. "Why did you come out here?"

"I just…couldn't sleep."

I wasn't buying it. "Why are you crying?"

"I'm not crying." She continued to hide her face, letting her hair cover her side profile.

"Don't lie to me. I don't lie to you."

She sniffed slightly then wiped her nose.

I leaned against the fence and rested my arm on top. I stared at the side of her face, waiting for her to look me in the eye. Up until that point, she'd never been afraid to meet my gaze. No matter how intimidating I was, she never flinched. But now her posture was broken, and she seemed defeated. "Muse."

"I don't want to talk about it."

"Why not?"

"I just don't." She scratched the horse behind the ears then stepped away. "I'll come inside now so you can go back to sleep."

I could just let the conversation die and return to bed, but I was too involved not to care. I didn't like those tears, not when they weren't caused by me. I didn't like knowing she was in pain, unless she was struggling to take my dick. Knowing there was something gnawing at her made me feel vulnerable too. "Muse." I grabbed her by the elbow and forced her to face me. "You can talk to me."

"You don't care, Conway. And that's fine. You don't need to pretend with me." She turned away again.

I grabbed her again, and this time, I dragged her into me. "Would I have asked if I didn't care?"

She didn't twist out of my grasp. She held my gaze, her watery eyes slowly drying. "I just had a nightmare. I had to get out of bed. Sweat was everywhere, and I couldn't breathe…in the dark, I kept seeing his face. My first instinct was to go to your room, but then I remembered your intolerance. So I thought of the place that makes me feel happy…which is this place." She crossed her arms over her chest and stared at the horses in their pens.

I wanted to ask what her nightmare was about, but I could connect the dots. "Do they happen often?"

"Not like this one…it just felt so real. He killed my brother…he touched me. It was bad." She ran her hands through her hair and closed her eyes, like she was fighting the memory from entering her brain again.

"I'm sorry." It wasn't an empty phrase to replace a real sentiment. I really felt terrible that she felt that way. I'd always considered Muse to be a strong woman, a fearless one who never gave up. To see her break down in fear made me feel like shit.

"Let's go back to the house." She turned away and hit the lights before we walked up the path.

Not once did she want me to hold her. Not once did she even let me touch her. She was closed off from me, keeping me at a distance because she didn't feel welcome to do anything else. She'd wanted to come to my room but assumed that was off-limits.

I didn't want to sleep with her, but this time, I wanted to make an exception.

I'd already made exceptions for her before anyway.

We walked back to the house, and I set the alarm once more.

"I'm sorry," she repeated. "I won't do it again." She walked to the stairs.

"Muse."

She stopped halfway up but didn't turn around.

I walked until I reached her at the same level. Her arms were still crossed over her chest, and she seemed so much smaller than usual. I didn't like this weak version of Muse.

I didn't like seeing her afraid, not when she had nothing to be afraid of. "Sleep with me."

Her eyes couldn't hide their surprise. "It's okay, Conway. But thank you." She kept walking and reached the second floor.

I walked with her. "I mean it."

"Really, it's fine." She reached the third floor then walked to her bedroom.

I preferred the moments when she wanted me, when she would dig her nails into my chest possessively. I preferred her kisses and her warmth to her coldness. She'd become closer to me as the months passed, and every time she got too comfortable, I hit the brakes and pushed her away. I reminded her that she was just a woman I owned, not a person I actually cared about.

But I reaped what I sowed.

And now she wasn't turning to me when she needed me.

I wanted her to need me. "Muse?"

This time, she didn't stop. "Good night, Conway." She walked inside her bedroom and shut the door behind her.

I stayed outside her door, knowing she'd given me a way out. I could just go to bed and forget this whole thing. I could enjoy my large bed alone and know she would get over this on her own. In the morning, we could both forget tonight ever happened.

It would be so easy.

But that was not what I wanted. I opened the door and walked inside.

Muse had already taken her boots and jeans off. Her back was to me as she pulled her plaid shirt over her head and tossed it on the ground. I hadn't visited her room often, but I noticed she was meticulously clean. There was never shoes or clothes on the ground. Her bathroom counters were always free of her makeup bag and her toothbrush. She cleaned up after herself like she was a guest in my home.

But she wasn't a guest. This was her home.

She grabbed a nightshirt from her drawer and pulled it over her head, keeping her back to me.

I knew she heard me, but she continued to ignore me.

I pulled my clothes off then got underneath her covers. It was a king bed like my own, with the same mattress and sheets. The only difference was the color of the bedding. Her room was decorated in pink and gold, and mine remained in masculine tones of gray, black, and brown.

When she turned around and looked at me, her surprise replaced her sadness. She stood in the long white t-shirt with her hair pulled over one shoulder. The puffiness of her eyes had gone down because the cool temperature decreased the swelling. But the devastation was still etched into her face, like carvings out of stone.

I pulled back the covers on her side. "Get in."

It seemed like she might try to argue with me, might try to

convince me that she didn't need me. But there was no argument, and she got into bed beside me. She stuck to her side, lying on her back and looking at the ceiling. Then she turned off the lamp.

I wrapped my arm around her waist and dragged her across the bed toward me.

She didn't fight me, but her breathing picked up.

I positioned her against my chest, pulling her arm across my stomach and yanking her leg across my waist. I combined us together until we were a single person, her cold body slowly becoming warm because of mine. I rested my lips against her forehead and ran my hand up her toned thigh.

After a minute, her body finally relaxed. Her hand gripped my side, and she released a quiet sigh. She adjusted her body a little before she was in the optimal position. Then she remained still, cuddled into my side.

I kissed her forehead and ran my fingers through her hair. She was the softest woman I'd ever touched, with hair like silk and skin like rose petals. She had the prettiest blue eyes, the kind I could get lost in when I fucked her. For someone so pretty, she was very fierce. She'd been through a lot and never allowed it to get to her. But this dream broke her, made her run into the night for comfort.

She'd wanted to run to me first.

"You never have to be scared as long as I'm living." I kept my lips against her forehead, letting my mouth brush against her skin as I spoke. "I will always protect you, Muse. I protect all my girls, but I'll protect you most of all."

Her fingers felt the grooves of my stomach. "I know."

"Then don't ever think about him. And you'll never dream about him."

"I don't," she whispered. "But I guess it's always lingering in the back of my mind."

"Don't allow it to."

"Do you think he'll come after me?"

According to the Underground rules, he couldn't. "No. We have rules for this sort of thing. If a master buys a slave, another master can't steal her away. Once the transaction is complete, he has ownership. Otherwise, it would undermine the business of the Skull Kings. No one will go to their auctions if men will just steal slaves from each other."

"I can't believe criminals have rules…"

"Rules are always necessary. So, if he broke them, he wouldn't be allowed to return to another auction."

"Yes…but he might not care."

Talking about this was only making her more upset. "Even if he doesn't, he can't cross me. It's not possible. Not only am I rich and famous, but I'm very powerful. Carter and I have eyes and ears everywhere. If he ever comes within ten miles of you, I'll know about it. Alright?"

She didn't speak.

"Alright?" I pressed.

"Alright."

I tilted her head back so we could see each other's eyes. I raised my head up and kissed her on the mouth, felt the heat between our lips. Ever since the first time I'd felt her mouth with mine, the chemistry had been powerful. I'd kissed women before, and it never felt the way it did with her.

Here I was, comforting this woman in her bed when I could have walked away. But I didn't want to brush it off and pretend it never happened. I wanted this woman to break her chains and be free.

She felt my mouth with hers, giving me purposeful kisses that were slow and sensual. Her hand glided into the back of my hair, and she felt the strands with her fingertips. Every time she touched me, my body lit on fire. I could feel the way she wanted me, the way her body responded to me on an innate level.

My cock hardened underneath her leg, ballooning up until it grew to its full size. I couldn't control my reactions to her. My cock had a mind of its own. When a beautiful woman like Muse was kissing me and touching me, there was nothing I could do to stop it.

But I didn't make a move, unsure if she wanted me to. It was one of the few times I let her make the decision. If I didn't care about her, I would just go for it. But I didn't want to be insensitive.

And she made the move.

She slowly rolled onto her back and pulled me with her.

My mouth wanted to kiss her harder, but I kept my kisses slow and purposeful. My hands wanted to rip her panties off, and I wanted to fold her underneath me so I could fuck her deep and hard. But that didn't feel right, so I resisted the urge.

She pulled my boxers to my knees then ran her hands up my back. She spoke against my mouth as she kept kissing me. "Make love to me…"

My mouth hesitated against hers for an instant as I processed what she said. I'd never made love to a woman in my life. It was all hard fucking and passionate screwing. It was about getting off, getting hot, sweaty, and satisfied.

But not that romantic bullshit.

I could tell her no. I had every right to do whatever I wanted. But I didn't.

I pulled her panties off then moved between her legs. My eyes locked on hers, and I separated her thighs with my knees before I pushed inside her. Even though she was emotional just minutes ago, she was wet for me when I felt her.

I pushed through her wetness then slid inside, moving slowly as I inched farther.

Her nails dug into my shoulders as she looked up at me, her lips slightly parted while her blue eyes were lit up like Christmas lights. She was such a sexy woman without even trying. If I could photograph her this way, my lingerie would always be out of stock.

But I didn't want to share her with the world.

She was mine.

I sank completely inside her until my balls touched her ass.

She took a deep breath, her tits rising until her nipples touched my chest.

I held myself over her and started to thrust, my lips brushing against hers as I kissed her softly. I rolled my hips with the movements, pushing all the way in before I pulled out again. Her pussy was so wet, so tight. She wasn't as tight as she was when I first took her, but she was still petite. I enjoyed that smallness, that tightness.

It felt incredible.

She breathed into my mouth heavier and harder, her ankles digging into my ass. Every time she took a deep breath, her nails cut into me a little harder. Her tits shook with my thrusts, and in the middle of her kiss, her lips would tremble.

I knew she was going to come. It was the quickest she'd ever had an explosion. It was the quickest she'd ever been pushed over the edge. This was how she wanted me, nice and slow. She wanted my affection as well as my cock. She wanted my intimacy, my adoration. Muse didn't care about my money or my wealth. All she wanted was me—the man underneath the suit.

She sucked my bottom lip into her mouth before she gave me her tongue. It was small and wet, and she touched it to mine and breathed at the same time.

Fuck, this was hot.

I never knew sex could be this good when it was this slow.

I felt her thighs squeeze against me and tremble. I felt her nipples harden even more against my chest. Her nails made small cuts into my skin, nearly drawing blood with their sharpness. Her pussy constricted, tightening around me even more.

Fuck, I already wanted to come.

Instead of concentrating on how quickly I could shove my dick inside her, I focused on her kiss and her touch. Those things were even more stimulating than the pussy wrapped around my dick. The wetness of her mouth was even better than the wetness of her cunt. I adored every feature she possessed, from her gorgeous legs to the beauty of her eyes. She was the sexiest woman on the planet, on the inside as well as the outside.

"Come for me." I needed her to explode. I needed her to finish. I couldn't be one of those assholes that didn't let their women go first. I'd never been that guy, and I didn't want to start being him now.

Especially to her.

She gripped my back and pulled me completely inside her, taking in my entire length so she could come all around me. She dug her nails into me and then exploded, whimpering against my mouth as she hit her high and glided back down again.

I held on as long as I could, enough to make sure she would enjoy every second of my thick dick. Then I came inside her a second later, exploding with a loud groan. I filled her with my come, feeling the satisfaction immediately spike in my veins. "Muse…" Her pussy was heaven to me, the only place I ever wanted to be. I buried my face into her neck as I finished, smelling her sweat as well as her perfume.

It was one of the best orgasms I'd ever had.

My dick softened, but I still felt the remains of the climax. My entire body felt tired and satisfied. My come was deep inside her, mixed with hers. I'd never been inside a woman so much in my life. I had a quick turnaround rate, but Muse had been the longest partner I'd ever had.

And I still wasn't tired of her.

I lay beside her and immediately closed my eyes, exhausted.

We were both sweaty, but she still moved into me and wrapped her leg over my hip. She cuddled into me and breathed a sigh of satisfaction.

I wrapped my arm around her waist, and I didn't have a single thought before I crashed.

I fell asleep, my arms enveloping this woman. And I slept well.

DANTE HAD breakfast set up in her living room, so I sat there and drank my coffee while I waited for her to wake up. The newspaper was open in my lap, and the view of the property was breathtaking from the window. The sun had risen over the horizon and blanketed the landscape in golden sunlight.

I had work to do that day, but I decided to blow it off.

I was needed elsewhere.

She opened the door from the bedroom and stood in the white t-shirt she put on last night. Her hair was a mess from the way I fisted it during the night, and her eyes held sleepy satisfaction. Her gaze narrowed slightly as she looked at me, obviously expecting me to be gone by now.

"Hungry?" I folded the newspaper and set it on my lap. I was in my black sweatpants with a bare chest. My feet rested on the soft carpet, and I felt the morning light enfold me in warmth. It was going to be a warm day, but I'd always loved the heat. Must be my Tuscan roots.

She sat on the couch across from me and picked up a mug of hot coffee. She pulled her knees to her chest and crossed her ankles.

But I caught a glimpse between her legs. She still didn't have any panties on.

Fuck.

Seeing that little slit first thing in the morning got my engine revving in a way my coffee didn't. I suspected my come was still sitting inside her, thick and warm. I wanted to hook a finger inside her just to check.

She sipped her coffee and looked out the window.

I turned back to the newspaper and reveled in the comfortable silence between us. I enjoyed times like these, when talking wasn't necessary. I'd never been much of a conversationalist. There were much better ways of communicating than through speech.

She grabbed her plate of scrambled eggs and bacon and ate quietly, her fork tapping lightly against the china.

I kept reading.

"Sleep well?"

I slept better than I ever had. "Yes. You?"

"Yes."

I didn't take my eyes off my paper.

"Are you going to work in Milan today?"

"No." I closed my paper and tossed it on the table. "I have other plans."

"Oh?"

"When you've finished your breakfast, get dressed. I'll meet you at the stables."

Surprise came over her face. "Why?"

"I'm going to show you a few things."

"You?" she asked. "Don't you have work to do?"

I knew I hadn't been the greatest man when it came to Muse. I treated her well, but not that well. I was cold to her when she didn't deserve it, and I didn't worship her in the way she did deserve. I guess I wanted to make that right. "Yes. But I'd rather spend time with you."

———

WE ARRIVED AT THE STABLES, both dressed for the dust and the heat.

"I can't picture you working out here." She looked adorable in her Stetson and denim jeans. They went high up her waist but hugged her body perfectly. She wore a white camisole with a plaid shirt over top. It was tied in the front, making the fabric hug the deep curve in her lower back.

I hadn't realized the word adorable was in my vocabulary until then.

"Just because I make clothes indoors doesn't mean I don't know how to work outdoors." I grabbed the saddle and reins for my horse and then carried it to Carbine's pen.

Muse watched me. "Are we going riding?"

"Yes."

The look she gave me was priceless. She looked happier than I'd ever seen her, as if her dream really had come true. "Really?"

"Yep."

She covered her mouth with both hands momentarily, her excitement uncontainable. "I've wanted to ride for months now."

"I think you're ready."

"Which horse am I going to ride on?"

"Carbine." I walked into his pen and set up his bridle.

"Really?" She stood on the outside of the gate and rested her hands on the wooden fence. "He's so volatile."

"Not with me." I rubbed his nose and tightened the leather. "He's a good horse. He'll take care of you." I held him by the reins and pulled him out of the pen and into the center of the stables. I tied him in place then got to work on the saddle.

Muse moved to the other side and started to help me.

Carbine snarled then stepped away from her.

I whistled. "Boy, no."

Muse stepped back and didn't approach him again. "Are you sure this is a good idea?"

"Yes." I secured the saddle then met Carbine face-to-face. I clicked my tongue then scratched him behind the ears. He was hostile because he was misunderstood. He only responded to people he recognized. While we were different species, we had the same personality. "Come here, Muse."

She slowly walked toward me.

"He likes to be rubbed right here." I placed her hand at the top of his head, right where his mane began to grow.

She scratched the area.

Carbine didn't move.

"He prefers to eat apples. He'll eat carrots once in a while, but he has a sweet tooth." I pulled a red apple out of the bag and handed it to her.

She fed it to him, and Carbine devoured it.

"I need you to treat this lady right, alright?" I spoke to my horse even though he didn't understand me, but he understood my moods. If I was particularly angry, he knew to stay away from me. If I was somber, he chased after me. He recognized my attitude, and I recognized his. We were both intuitive.

I pulled him into the riding pen with Muse behind me. "Always approach him on the right side, not the left."

"Why?"

I shrugged. "He doesn't like it. That's all I know."

She followed my directions.

I came up behind her and grabbed her by the hips. "Right foot in the stirrup first."

She secured her boot inside.

"Then pull your weight up onto the saddle by the horn. Don't move slowly. The quicker you launch yourself, the easier it'll be."

She pulled herself over quickly, getting herself in the saddle without issue. She grabbed the reins and scooted closer to the horn. She ran her fingers through Carbine's mane and stared down at him. "I never thought this was possible. He wouldn't even let me feed him."

"He's not as hostile as he seems. He just puts up a front." I stepped back against the fence. "Now walk him in a circle."

"When are we going to go on a long ride?" she asked. "You know, over a trail or something?"

Like always, she wanted to jump ahead. While her excitement was infectious, it was rushed. "Basics first. Then we'll talk."

―――――

WE HAD lunch then afternoon sex. She was on top, riding and grinding me better than Carbine. Then she fell asleep in my bed, so I showered and got ready for my plans that evening. I was meeting Carter at my lingerie club.

We hadn't spoken in weeks.

I put on a dark blue suit and matching tie before I slipped my shiny watch onto my wrist. My shoes had been shined, and the clothing fit me as well as my lingerie fit my models. To most people, a suit was just uncomfortable clothing that squeezed your neck and weighed you down. People didn't understand it was a non-violent weapon. Intimidation kept people at bay.

When I walked back into my bedroom, Muse was sitting up in bed with the sheets pulled up to her chest. Her hair was messy like before because I'd screwed it up again when I fisted it in my hand.

She looked me up and down. "Where are you going?"

"I'm meeting Carter."

"Oh."

I grabbed my phone off the dresser and dropped it into my pocket.

"When will you be back?"

My natural instinct was to tell her it was none of her business. She didn't have the right to ask me questions, as if my decisions were any of her concern. But I was training myself not to be such an ass. "Later tonight."

"Can I come along?"

I was going to the lingerie club, where every woman who wanted admission had to be dressed in lingerie. I didn't want Muse half naked in front of anyone, even if my arm was wrapped around her shoulders. "It's a business meeting."

She finally let it go. "Alright."

I sat on the bed beside her and leaned in to kiss her. A part of me didn't want to leave her, not after the day we'd spent together. I knew she was still vulnerable after that nightmare. I wanted to fix everything for her, make her feel safe.

"I'd like to sleep with you again tonight…if that's alright." She pressed her forehead against mine.

I didn't want her to get comfortable around me, to expect things from me. But it was still too soon to be a jerk. After making her smile all day, I didn't want to take that away. I could undo all the work I'd just done with the snap of a finger. "Yes."

"Okay."

I kissed her on the forehead before I walked out. I took my Ferrari to Milan and parked it in my building before I walked up the street to the club. I preferred to leave my car in the garage so it wouldn't get scratches from the idiots who drove shitty cars and didn't give a damn about mine.

The bouncers held everyone back as I stepped inside, walking into the world I owned. The Barsetti line owned various businesses in different capacities. It was the best way to protect assets, by diversifying into different sectors.

The women stared at me as I passed, recognizing me instantly. Whenever I was there, women always made a pass at me, whether they wanted to spend the night with me or they wanted to convince me to give them a shot on the runway. Pictures of my most famous girls were on the walls, Lacey Lockwood having the largest spotlight.

If Muse were on display, no one would give a damn about Lacey Lockwood.

But Muse was just for me to enjoy.

I found my private booth on the second landing, the place where no one else was allowed to go besides Carter and me.

Carter already had two women to entertain him, one under each arm. They wore black lingerie, their tits popping out and their thongs barely covering anything down below.

I sat across from him and watched the waitress set a glass of scotch in front of me. "Carter."

One of the women kissed his neck as she pressed her tits into his chest.

"Conway. How's it going?"

"Good. I can tell you're having a good evening." The waitress set a tray in front of me along with a lit cigar. I immediately picked it up and took a drag. I didn't smoke cigars often, but they were my weakness. They took the edge off in a way booze couldn't. It was soothing down into my lungs.

"I'm always having a good evening." He waved the women away. "Give us a minute, ladies."

Like obedient dogs, they scurried away.

If I said that to Muse, she would give me a glare and not move. The thought made me smile.

"What are you smirking about?" Carter placed a cigar in his mouth and lit it. Smoke came from the tip and drifted into the air.

"Nothing. What's new?"

"I haven't gotten any new clients. But I deposited the cash for Anastasia into your account."

"I saw that."

"I'll wait until I hear something new. At least we can have a break."

I didn't want to go back to the Underground. It was easy money, but after seeing Muse tied up there and naked, I didn't want to step back inside. I had the money to get her out of there, but what about the others? They were sold into horrific lives and even more gruesome deaths. I never thought about it deeply until it came to Muse. Once I pictured her in chains, it started to feel real. "I'm not sure if I want to go back anyway."

"Why?"

All I did was shake my head.

"I can't show my face there. You know that."

I sucked on my cigar.

"How's your prisoner? My father told me she's lovely."

"Because she is lovely." She was gorgeous, on the inside

and the outside. Not once did she ask me to buy her expensive clothes or jewelry. In her free time, she worked in the stables and made herself useful. She tried to pay back the money I spent on her, even though it would take twenty lifetimes to do it. She was hardworking and honorable. She wasn't afraid to have dirt under her nails or sweat on her chest.

The corner of his mouth rose in a smile. "And he mentioned you had a little make-out session with her in his club."

"If it bothers him, he shouldn't watch."

Carter ignored my comment. "What happened to the no-kissing policy?"

All I did was stare at him and enjoy my cigar.

"You like your little prisoner?"

She wasn't a prisoner. She asked me to sleep with her, asked me to make love to her. She called me her friend and confided in me. "I don't mind her."

"My father said your parents really like her."

I exhaled the smoke and let it float toward the ceiling. "She's pretty likable."

"And Vanessa and she are friends?"

"Vanessa is just a loser who's desperate for attention."

He chuckled because he knew that wasn't true. "Con, it's

okay if you like the girl. I've seen her, and she's pretty damn beautiful."

He was my cousin and my friend, so I knew he would never cross me. That was the only reason he was allowed to make that statement. "I enjoy her, yes. But that's the extent of it."

"Then why are you introducing her to your parents?"

Because Muse was as smart as she was pretty. "I told her to stay in her room, but she tricked me. She came downstairs and talked to my mom and sister while my father and I were at the stables. By the time I returned, the damage had been done. Now I have to go along with the charade. And if I don't give her what she wants, she'll tell my family what our relationship really is."

"What does she want?"

A lot of things. "Me."

"Meaning?"

"My affection, friendship, and gentleness. She doesn't want to be bossed around or treated like a prisoner. She wants me to treat her with respect. I've done all those things."

He chuckled. "Smart girl."

"It's not so bad. She's pleasant company."

He enjoyed his cigar and kept staring at me, his eyes studying my face. "You love her?"

I shot him a glare.

"I'm serious."

"I don't. Our relationship isn't romantic. It's just…physical."

"You said there was friendship and affection as well…the foundation of romance."

"Not for us," I said. "I treat her well, but it doesn't change the relationship. I own her, and she's my property. That's it."

"Are you monogamous?"

"No."

He nodded slowly. "Then it's not romantic. Does she get mad when you sleep with other women?"

I hadn't slept with anyone since the day I laid eyes on her. I hadn't even been attracted to anyone else. Anytime I was hard, I was hard for her. When I designed lingerie, she inspired every piece. So far, there'd only been room for one woman in my mind. "She's a jealous woman."

"Then maybe she loves you."

I hadn't considered it. I knew she respected me and was attracted to me. She was grateful I saved her, and she thought I was a hero. But love…I didn't think that was possible. I bought her like livestock and used her like property. She might enjoy my company and want me in her bed, but that didn't mean she loved me. I didn't deserve the love of a woman like that, so she would never give it to me. "Unlikely."

"If she likes sleeping with you and enjoys your company, then she must."

"She's just grateful I saved her life. If I hadn't, this arrangement would be completely different."

"Then why does she get angry when you sleep with other women?" He grinned as he backed me into a corner. "That's all the evidence you need."

"She gets jealous when I'm around the models, but I haven't actually slept with anyone, so I'm not sure what her reaction would be."

Carter was about to take another drag from his cigar, but he steadied his hand. "Hold up. You haven't slept with anyone else in…two months?"

I shrugged. "I guess."

"Con, that means you're in a relationship."

"No, it doesn't. I told her I would sleep with other women. The opportunity just hasn't come up because I've been so busy."

"Uh-huh."

I drank my scotch. "I don't give a damn what you think, Carter."

"If that's the case, why don't you just admit what this really is?"

There was nothing to admit. I enjoyed Muse in many ways, and there was nothing wrong with that. The only reason I hadn't fucked anyone was because it hadn't come up. If I saw a sexy woman I wanted, I would have her. I'd take someone back to my apartment tonight if I wanted to. "Lay off, Carter."

"Lay off, huh?" He snapped his fingers and got the attention of the women again.

They walked back to us, both brunettes and both curvy in all the right places. Either one could qualify to be one of the models on my runway. Both were beautiful, with pretty hair and glowing skin.

"Pick one." Carter kept his eyes on me. "I'll take the other."

"I can get my own girl, asshole."

"If not her, then pick whoever you want. Prove to me this woman doesn't mean anything to you."

"Why do you care, Carter?" Whether I liked the woman or not, it shouldn't matter to him. We were friends and we were family. But my personal life shouldn't be that interesting to him.

"I care because I don't want you to lie to yourself. And you do that a lot."

I hated to be overanalyzed, especially when the other person was right. "I'm not, Carter."

He snapped his fingers again. "Then Cassandra is yours for the night. And Berenice is mine."

CARTER and I were close in age, so we'd always gotten along more like brothers than cousins. Our fathers weren't just brothers, but best friends. I saw him every weekend, and we were inseparable for most of our childhood.

So picking up women together was pretty normal.

Cassandra was a stripper at a downtown club, and she told me about life working in bars. Her hands were usually on my body, and she snuck a kiss or two. She eventually scooted onto my lap.

Carter was lost in Berenice, his finger hooked into her thong at her hip. She ground against him as they kissed on the leather sofa.

I wanted to prove Carter wrong, but I realized it wasn't so simple.

I wasn't into this at all.

Right now, I should have a hard-on. A gorgeous woman was sitting on my lap, and the second I asked if she wanted to get out of there, she would say yes.

She was beautiful, sexy, and experienced. She'd do anything I asked. If I snapped my fingers, she'd be on her knees sucking me off.

But anytime I pictured the fantasy, Muse was the one on her knees.

She was the only one I wanted.

I wanted to prove a point, but it seemed childish to sleep with this woman when I didn't even want to.

But I didn't want Carter to be right.

And I certainly didn't want to be wrong.

The sexiest woman in the world was waiting at home for me. She turned to me for strength and for protection. She kissed me like I was the only man she cared about. I was the only man she'd ever been with. Her pussy was untouched—except by me.

Now Cassandra started to kiss my neck and run her hand up my thigh. She was searching for my hard-on through my slacks.

But she wouldn't find it.

My lack of arousal had nothing to do with this woman's charms. The guilt was overwhelming. I felt like I was doing something wrong even though I wasn't. Muse was waiting at home for me, still afraid of that nightmare she had. Until I was by her side, she wouldn't truly feel safe from Knuckles.

And I was in a club, pretending to enjoy myself.

I couldn't do this, not even to save face. "I'm sorry, sweetheart. I just remembered I have to be somewhere." I gently pushed her off my lap and rose to a stand.

Carter pulled his tongue out of the other woman's mouth to give me a grin. "Looks like I proved my point."

"I really do have to be somewhere."

"I know," he said smugly. "And we both know where."

I walked out of the club and got into my car in the garage. Carter and I had talked about a few things, but nothing that really interested me. I didn't even have the opportunity to ask about Knuckles because we were too busy talking about Muse.

I gripped the steering wheel on the drive home. My knuckles were turning white as the anger throbbed in the vein in my neck. Instead of spending the evening enjoying booze, cigars, and women, I was too busy feeling guilty. Sitting in that club was the last place I wanted to be. I wanted to go home, to be with the woman who was waiting for me.

How the fuck did I get here?

It was pathetic.

She wasn't supposed to mean anything to me. I wasn't supposed to like her. I wasn't supposed to take the day off to cheer her up. I should be sinking between a woman's legs right now—preferably two.

But I was on my way back to Muse.

I'd never felt like such a pussy.

Forty minutes later, I pulled into the roundabout and left my keys on the dash. I walked inside my three-story mansion and was greeted by Dante. He gave me a slight nod before he went outside to take care of the car.

My suit needed to be dry cleaned now that it smelled like booze, cigars, and a woman's perfume. I stripped off the jacket and loosened the tie on my way to my bedroom. I passed Muse's on the way then stepped into the privacy of my room. I threw my jacket on the couch then yanked the tie from my collar. I tossed that aside too, knowing Dante would find it in the morning.

"How was your night?"

I recognized her voice immediately, the sultry depth that filled my fantasies. It was soothing all the way down my spine, gliding across my skin and making all the muscles in my body tense. A beautiful woman had been sitting on my lap all night, and my cock never sprang into action. But the second I heard her voice, my slacks tightened. She had an unbelievable power over me. All she had to do was speak and I wanted her.

How did this happen?

I couldn't enjoy a night out the way I used to. I couldn't get lost in passionate sex with a woman I wouldn't remember the next day. The only woman on my mind was the one standing behind me. Ever since she walked into my life, my world had been turned upside down. I paid a fortune just to protect her, and now I was chasing away her nightmares like a damn teddy bear.

How did I get here?

"Everything alright?"

I turned around when I finally had the strength to face her. I was hard in my slacks, and the second my eyes settled on her, my cock thickened even more. There was no piece of lingerie that could compete with one of my t-shirts. Seeing it loose around her body as it stretched to her knees was the biggest turn-on in the world. I'd never been so aroused by a woman, never wanted to plow a woman so deeply into my mattress before. Her long hair trailed down her shoulders, and she wore a sleepy expression as she looked at me. Without a drop of makeup, her face was completely natural.

She didn't even need makeup.

That was how beautiful this woman was.

I hated my weakness for her. I hated the way she chased away my anger with just a simple expression.

It made me angrier. "It's fine." I wasn't in the mood to talk. Now I was in the mood to lay her at the foot of my bed and give it to her deep and good.

She crossed the distance between us, leaving the doorway and approaching me near the couch. Her small feet tapped lightly against the rug. Her hands reached me first, touching my opened shirt. She rose on her tiptoes to move into me, clearly missing me since the second I was gone.

Fuck. Me.

My hand moved into the back of her hair, and I kissed her, kissed her the way I'd never kissed anyone else. I sucked her bottom lip then gave her my tongue right in the beginning. Her perfume surrounded me, and I couldn't wait until that smell was mixed with the scent of sex. My hand moved underneath the t-shirt, and I felt her soft skin, moving up her waistline until I cupped one of her firm tits.

Perfect.

She was so fucking perfect.

I didn't want to wait until I made it into the bedroom. The couch would do just fine. I guided her backward as I loosened my slacks and pushed them down along with my boxers.

She shoved my shirt off my shoulders then lay back, her eyes glowing with anticipation. This inexperienced woman had been terrified of me once before, but now she yearned for sex the way I did. She couldn't get enough of it—couldn't get enough of me. She lifted her legs and pressed her feet against my chest.

I pulled her thong down her legs then tossed it aside. My cock was raging, and I was anxious. I'd been out all night trying to chase something I didn't even want. What I wanted was right here underneath me.

I moved between her legs and felt my warm cock slide through her wet folds.

She'd wanted me long before I walked through the door.

I held myself over her then pinned one of her legs to the back of the couch. My breathing picked up in excitement.

I'd been balls deep in that pussy before, but every time felt like the first time.

Her hands glided up my chest, but then they stopped abruptly. The desire in her eyes immediately disappeared, and a look of pain stretched across her face. That didn't last long either before she looked angrier than I'd ever seen her. "Asshole." Without warning, she slapped her palm across my face as hard as she could.

I turned my face slightly with the hit, feeling the redness and sting instantaneously. She hit me hard enough to leave a handprint, I was certain. The action didn't hurt, but the surprise caught me off guard.

She shoved me in the chest, but I didn't move because I was too heavy. She shoved me again then gave up and slipped out from underneath me. "Your little whores weren't enough for you? Then you come home to me and want more? Without even a shower first? You're a real piece of shit, Conway."

I got off the couch, my cock still hard because I found her just as arousing when she was angry as when she was happy. "Muse—"

"Don't call me that," she hissed. "You're covered with lipstick marks, you smell like a woman, and you taste like booze."

I hadn't considered the places where Cassandra had kissed me. I'd been too busy thinking about Muse even to notice. I could have wiped myself off with a tissue or sprayed on more cologne, but I hadn't been thinking.

She shook her head, her eyes narrowed in disappointment. "I've been waiting around for you all night. You hold me, kiss me, and you spend all day with me. For a moment, it seems like you actually care about me. But then you lie to me and go chase tail when I'm right here. I don't understand you, Conway. How can you tell me I'm the most desirable woman in the world but then want someone else?"

I didn't want anyone else. The terrifying truth was becoming more apparent with every passing day.

The disappointment in her eyes was heavy, like she'd never hated me more.

All I had to do was correct her, but I couldn't. I refused to give this woman anything. I refused to let her think I was faithful to her. If I did…then what would that mean? Where would that lead us? She meant nothing to me, and I had to keep it that way. I was pissed off that I even wanted to tell her the truth.

I didn't owe her anything.

It needed to stay that way.

"You are just a commodity I paid for, Muse," I said coldly. "You don't mean a damn thing to me, and you never will. I will go out and fuck as many women as I want, and you'll accept that. You'll spread your legs when I get home and fuck me like always. That's what I paid for—and you'll deliver."

A frigid look stretched over her face. She'd never stared at me that way before. She wasn't just angry, but disappointed. If she'd had any power, she would have used it against me right then. If she were strong, she'd beat her fists against my chest. She wanted to destroy me in that moment, but knew she had no weapon that could defeat me. She was weak and at my mercy. All she could do was take it. "Be careful what you wish for."

7

Sapphire

Conway was an enigma.

How could he take time off work to teach me to ride Carbine if he didn't care about me? How could he sleep with me and chase away my nightmares if I meant nothing to him? How could he kiss me but not anyone else?

Maybe I gave him too much credit.

Maybe he'd been right from the beginning.

He wasn't evil, but he wasn't good either.

I knew I wasn't just upset about his promiscuity. I was upset that I didn't mean more to him. Living with him every single day forced me to enjoy his company. I enjoyed watching his concentration as he worked, and I enjoyed talking with him over dinner. I even enjoyed the sex. Last time he was in my bed, I asked him to make love to me—and he did. I wasn't even sure why I asked that. I wasn't sure why his presence chased away my fear.

But it did.

And knowing he wanted to be with some other woman after the connection we created hurt.

It hurt a lot.

But I wasn't going to let him hurt me anymore. There wasn't much I could do about my current situation. I was stuck there for the indefinite future. But I needed to lock away my vulnerability and never let him hurt me again. If he wanted to be with other women, then he couldn't have all of me.

Not anymore.

I was afraid I would catch something, but there wasn't much I could do about that either. I just hoped he wore a condom. He didn't seem like an idiot who wouldn't.

I didn't sleep that night and went to the stables in the morning. Marco was there, and he talked to me about the horses and work that needed to be done. He never mentioned my personal relationship with Conway, probably because he knew the subject was off-limits.

But that was refreshing.

I worked harder than usual to burn off my angry energy. I cleaned all the stalls, moved the hay, and groomed the horses before I worked in the barn. It was a sweltering day in the heat, and the back of my shirt was soaked with sweat. But the intense conditions didn't bother me.

I showered at the end of the day and changed my clothes before I took a packed dinner back to the stables and ate in the grass near Carbine's pen. The stars were bright up above because we were in the countryside. The closest house was over a mile away, so there were no lights to obstruct the view.

I ate my dinner then lay back in the grass so I could stare at the sky. It was still warm even though the sun had been gone for hours. The grass was soft, and I could hear Carbine release a snort here and there. He eventually walked toward me and stuck his head over the rail to look at me.

My gaze shifted to his snout. "Looks like you're finally warming up to me."

Hot breath reached my face.

"I'd give you something to eat, but I already ate everything."

He released a quiet neigh.

Sometimes, it seemed like the horse really understood what I was saying. I shifted my gaze back to the stars and wondered about my life. Just months ago, everything was normal. I was a student working in a bar. I focused on my studies then went out with friends on the weekends. I was grateful I had my mother's house because I couldn't afford rent in the city. But then Nathan got lost in booze and gambling and made the gravest mistake of his life—something that ruined my life.

Now I was on the other side of the world, living a completely different life.

Thankfully, Italy was beautiful. Otherwise, this would be a completely different experience. And if Conway weren't such a beautiful man, my situation would be different too.

My eyes grew heavy as I stared at the sky. Slowly, my eyelids started to fall. Under the stars on the soft grass, I drifted off into a peaceful sleep.

"MUSE." His deep and irritated voice woke me from my dreams.

My eyes snapped open, and I looked up into the darkness to see Conway's silhouette.

"What the hell are you doing out here? You had me worried."

"I'm surprised," I answered like a smartass. "I didn't think assholes worried about anything." I grabbed the bag Dante packed for me and stood up. I couldn't see Conway's face, but I assumed he was glaring at me.

His silence showed his anger.

I started back toward the house.

Conway followed behind me. "I don't care what you do on the property, but don't be careless."

"I'm just as safe out here as I am in the house."

"Not when I don't know where you are." He walked beside me, dressed in jeans and a t-shirt. He stared at me on the walk, his thick arms by his sides.

"Don't pretend you give a shit about me, Conway. We both know you don't." I increased my pace to put distance between us. I got to the house first and went to my bedroom upstairs, doing my best to avoid him. I didn't even want to look at his face right now. Anytime I did, I pictured the woman he was with last night. She probably had brown hair and bright eyes. She was probably gorgeous and thrilled she got to sleep with the amazing Conway Barsetti. Smoke practically exploded out of my nostrils.

Maybe I was jealous.

I made it inside my room and pulled off my tight jeans and boots. My plaid shirt was covered with stalks of grass, and I smelled like the outdoors.

My door opened and Conway stepped inside.

"Do I need to teach you how to knock?" I was in my panties and bra, my socks still on my feet. I didn't look at him as I tossed the dirty clothes into the hamper for Dante to collect in the morning.

"Would you have let me in if I did?"

We both knew the answer to that one. I opened a drawer and pulled out a t-shirt. I wasn't self-conscious about my body in front of him, not when he'd seen me so many times. But I didn't want to give him a reason to fuck me tonight. I was still so pissed at him. The idea of those lips on mine made me want to hurl. I didn't want to kiss his skin, not when some other woman had done the same. I'd never assumed Conway was a saint, but now I viewed him in a whole different light. He didn't owe me anything, but I still expected something from him. Now I was disappointed in him. I'd thought he was a better man. Guess I was wrong.

He stepped closer to me, his green eyes bright against his tanned skin. He'd shaved that morning, but the shadow of new hair growth was starting to sprinkle his chin. He stopped inches away from me, wearing an expression I'd seen hundreds of times.

He wanted me.

I pulled my shirt over my head and covered my body. I didn't want that heated stare any longer. I used to feed on it, used to feel beautiful because of it. But now, I felt like one of the many. The second he was finished, I wouldn't be in his thoughts anymore. I should be grateful he went out of his way to be gentle with me, especially for my first time, but it was hard to feel grateful when I was hurt.

No, I was crushed.

He moved toward me then placed his hands on my hips. His fingertips pressed into the cotton of my shirt, the pressure igniting my senses. Instantly, I felt my body come alive. I could smell his cologne, feel his arousal, and sense his desire. Naturally, my body prepared to take him because that's what it wanted. I had been so eager for him last night, fantasizing about his kiss and his touch. I'd never gotten the release from that moment.

Looked like my body had more power than my mind.

He pressed his forehead to mine and brought me closer into him.

I wanted to fight it because he hurt me. But fighting it would only prolong the inevitable. I could take a stand, but that stand wouldn't last long. My situation wouldn't change, not unless I came up with a hundred million dollars to pay my debt to Conway. And even then, I would still need more money to pay Knuckles, along with my other bills.

I was stuck.

May as well make the best of it.

He moved his hand into my hair, and he tilted my face, forcing me to look at him. "I know you're mad at me, but I want you. I've wanted you all night and all day." His fingertips slid under the fall of my hair, and his hand inched underneath my shirt to my stomach.

He made me melt with just those simple words. I wanted to submit, and not just to please him, but to please myself. If I took the emotional heartache out of the picture, I knew I would need sex while living there. Conway was the sexiest man I'd ever seen, so if I could pick anyone, it would be him. Perhaps I needed to accept my circumstances instead of trying to make it mean something. It was just casual sex, meaningless and empty.

When I didn't pull away, he leaned in to kiss me.

I turned my face away, giving him my cheek and hiding my lips.

No kissing. If this was just casual fucking, then no kissing. Kissing meant a lot more to me than anything else, so that was off the table. It was the only way I could protect my feelings. I always grew weak in the knees when his lips were on mine. It was when I felt most connected to him, felt the emotion in my heart.

I would never kiss him again.

I pulled my shirt over my head then unclasped my bra.

Conway's eyes roamed over my body, the heat entering his gaze.

"You can have some of me. But you can't have all of me." I pulled my thong down next, then moved to the bed. I turned my back to him, not wanting to look at his face. I crawled on the bed, my position on all fours.

His jeans hit the ground, and he yanked his shirt over his head. He came up behind me, and when his knees hit the mattress, it sank. He inched closer to me then grabbed my hips. He leaned over me and pressed kisses to my spine.

I didn't want that either. "Don't kiss me, Conway."

His breaths fell onto my skin, the heat and moisture gliding down my spine. He rested his forehead against the back of my neck, but he restrained from pressing his full lips against my warm skin.

He put his weight on the balls of his feet then gripped my hips as he positioned me against him.

I stared straight ahead, waiting for his massive cock to move inside me.

He pointed his head at my entrance and then pushed. My slickness lubricated my channel, and he glided inside without resistance. He inched all the way into me until he was completely sheathed. An audible moan escaped his lips.

I bit my bottom lip so I'd stay quiet.

He pulled on my hips as he thrust into me at the same time, moving deep and hard every time. His thick cock stretched me apart, and his length hit me in the right spot every time. His pace was perfect, giving it to me at a regular rhythm that ignited the fire inside me.

A part of me wished I could look at him, to see his powerful body flex and tighten as he moved. But another part of me didn't want to see that sexy expression in his eyes, see the way he enjoyed me. It would only make me enjoy him even more…and that was the last thing I wanted.

His breathing intensified, and his cock thickened noticeably. His fingertips dug into my ass as he squeezed the muscle. I'd fucked him enough times to know when he was about to come. Right now, he was fighting it so I could go first.

He grabbed a fistful of hair and yanked, forcing my head back. He slammed into me harder, hitting me even more perfectly in the right spot. He went balls deep every time, his thrusts accompanied by masculine grunts. "Muse, come for me."

My body tightened, and the heat rushed through my fingertips. I knew the pleasure was fast approaching. Even when I tried to keep him at a distance, my body couldn't fight the goodness between my legs. Conway had an invisible power over me, the control of my reactions no matter how much I tried to fight them.

He fucked me harder.

Once I hit my threshold, there was no stopping it. I gripped the sheets with my fingertips, and I came all around his dick, sheathing him with my orgasm. "God…" It felt as good as all the other explosions. Only this man could make me feel this way, could hurt me so much, but still make me feel so good. "Yes…" I loved the way he pulled my hair and slammed into me at the same time.

He only lasted long enough for me to finish before he released with a moan, filling my pussy with all of his come. His hips bucked a few times at the end, his pumps becoming less and less. He shoved his dick completely inside me as he finished, making sure I got every single drop of his seed.

He leaned over me and pressed his face into the back of my hair. His chest was coated with sweat, and it clung to my back. He breathed into my hair, his cock slowly softening inside me. He caught his breath before he moved off me and lay beside me on the bed. He stared at the ceiling with his lidded eyes as his dick lay against his stomach.

It was tempting to lie beside him and relax, but the last thing I wanted was to snuggle with him. Now, this was just sex—and it would stay that way. I got off the bed, feeling his come shift inside me.

He propped himself on one elbow so he could look at me. "Where are you going?"

I didn't turn around to look at him. "I'm going to take a shower. Good night, Conway." Even if he wanted to sleep with me, I wouldn't let that happen. He couldn't have it both ways. He couldn't have a relationship with me unless he was loyal to me. If he wanted it to be casual, then it would be casual.

I walked into the bathroom and locked the door behind me so there wouldn't be any surprises. I got under the hot water and washed away his touch. I used to love the feeling of his seed inside me, but now I couldn't stand it. It made me sick to my stomach because I wondered if he did the same with all the others.

I didn't want to be one of the others.

I wanted to be different.

MY LIFE TURNED INTO A ROUTINE. I woke up early every morning and worked in the stables. Sometimes there wasn't much to do, so I kept myself busy by finding other things that needed to be fixed.

Marco started to run out of stuff to do because I'd become self-sufficient.

When I returned to the house, I showered and asked Dante to bring dinner to my room. My plan was to avoid Conway at all costs until I didn't have a choice. We didn't have anything in common anyway. There wasn't much to talk about.

And we certainly weren't friends.

I was just about to head to the stables a week later when Conway appeared at my bedroom door.

Already dressed in my tight jeans and boots, I stared at him. My plaid shirt was tied around my waist so I could get a breeze along my torso. One hand rested on the door as I stared directly into his eyes, seeing the indifferent expression he always wore.

He continued to stare.

And I refused to speak.

His eyes roamed over my face, taking in my features like he was trying to memorize them. When his eyes settled on my lips, he spoke. "I'm working in the studio today. I want you there."

I couldn't refuse the request, not when being his muse was my entire purpose. "Let me change, and I'll be there."

"No need to change." He stepped away from the door. "You're just going to take it off anyway." He headed down the hallway to the next corridor where his home studio was located.

I stood there for a moment, digesting his words in silence. Throughout the week, he'd stopped by my room for sex. But that's all it was. We fucked, and then he went to his room. There was no kissing or touching. There wasn't cuddling when it was over.

Straight sex.

I followed behind him and entered his studio. His fabrics were organized, and his mannequin stood in the center with pins pressed into the material. The black rope piece he'd been working on hung on a hanger.

I felt the piece of lingerie in my fingertips, my thumb gliding over the nylon. It was simple but extremely sexy. It was one of my favorite pieces he'd ever created. It was difficult to believe I was the inspiration for it. "What are you working on now?"

"I haven't sketched anything new lately. But I have some older ideas I wanted to create." He opened his notebook. On each page was a different creation. He signed them and dated them in the top corner. The page he had the book open to had been sketched two weeks ago.

"What's this one?"

"The Queen."

"The Queen?" I asked.

"Yes." He pointed to the fabric in the picture with a pencil. "Light pink fabric here. Bead of white here." He pointed to another section. "Rose gold pendant here." He pointed to the opening of the fabric. "It opens here and there."

It was a great piece. The color hinted at an inexperienced woman, but someone who would grow into her power. The combination of champagne pink, white, and rose gold showcased a feminine collection of power. "It's beautiful." I wondered when it was inspired, but I didn't ask because it wouldn't matter.

He got to work and grabbed the first piece of fabric.

I stripped down to my thong, standing barefoot in the slightly cold room. A robe was hanging on the coat hanger by the door, so I pulled it over my shoulders. When I turned around, I saw Conway looking at me.

Once my skin was concealed, he got back to work.

I sat in the chair and watched him, leaving him to concentrate in silence. Now that we didn't talk anymore, I didn't feel like I knew him. He came to my room for sex, and we didn't exchange a single word. Today was the longest conversation we'd had in over a week.

He kept working, cutting the fabric before he began to create his design. He started with the foundation first, getting the base of the fabric before he moved to the intricate design he had sketched out. "Marco tells me he's getting bored."

My eyes focused on his hands, watching his callused fingertips work the piece. "Yeah, I can tell."

"You need to take it down a notch. There's other things for you to do here."

"Such as?"

"The pool, the gym, the library…many things." His eyes never left his work. "Marco enjoys your company, but pretty soon, you're going to put him out of a job."

The last thing I wanted was for Marco to lose his retirement. He enjoyed his work, enjoying being outside with the horses while getting his hands dirty. He was connected to the Italian soil. "I don't want that to happen."

"Then take it easy." His shoulders remained straight as he worked, and his posture was perfect. When his hands moved, the intricate muscles in his forearms shifted. It was no surprise he had such corded muscles and arms with the intricate work he did.

I didn't want to do anything else, but since there was only so much work to be done, I couldn't take it away from Marco. But then an idea popped into my mind. "What if we expanded?"

"What does that mean?"

"What if we got more horses? What if we got some chickens so we could have fresh eggs?"

"I'm not interested in having a farm."

"Or cows and goats. I could use the milk to make cheese."

"Again, not interested. I already paid a fortune for you. I don't want to spend more money so you can have an expensive hobby."

"It wouldn't just be a hobby. I could sell everything we make at a local market."

"Because I need more money," he snapped. He didn't break his concentration even though his tone rose.

I couldn't override him when he made excellent points. He did pay a lot of money for me so he shouldn't spend another dime to make me happy. "I need something, Conway. Without a purpose, I'll be unhappy."

He sighed as he started to sew the fabric together.

"Let me work with you in Milan. I can do more than just inspire you."

"You aren't modeling."

That was another insult that burned. He wanted to keep me all to himself, but he couldn't keep his dick in his pants. It made no sense. "I have two years of business classes under my belt. I can help you do other things."

"You don't need a business degree to run a business. You need experience."

"Then let me have experience."

This time, he ignored me. His gaze was downturned on

his work. The concentration on his face was innately sexy. It reminded me of the nights he thrust between my legs. His eyes were on me, and he possessed me with just a look.

We sat together in silence for another twenty minutes. The sewing machine worked to fuse together the lines of fabric. Conway worked effortlessly, doing something innately complicated without appearing even slightly stressed.

There was a gnawing feeling in my stomach, something that haunted me every single day. I never asked because I knew he wouldn't answer. But I needed to know the truth, or it would eat me alive. "Conway, I need to know something. You have to answer me. I deserve the truth."

It was the first time he stopped working. He took his foot off the pedal and locked his gaze with mine.

"You wear something when you're with the others?"

His expression didn't change at all. He held my gaze without blinking, completely indifferent in response to my question.

"Conway," I pressed. "I deserve to know."

He turned his eyes back to his work. "You don't need to worry about catching anything, Muse. So drop it."

"I'm not going to drop it until I get an answer."

"I just told you you don't need to worry about it."

"Is that a yes?"

The sewing machine came back on, and he finished his task.

I let it go because I wouldn't get anything else out of him. He said I didn't need to worry about it, so hopefully, that meant he was safe. He seemed too smart to catch something from a complete stranger. I had to hope my assumption was right.

He carried the piece to the mannequin and hung it up on the artificial body. The pink color was perfect under the light, and the cut of the fabric was exact. It was amazing he had created something in such a short amount of time.

"Do you sew the design directly into the fabric?"

"I'll make a separate piece then stitch it directly on top."

"Interesting…"

He sat down again and got to work.

I flipped through his notebook and looked at his different sketches. From the very beginning until the present time there was a distinct evolution. I could tell when he met me just by looking at his art. There was a noticeable shift in his design. "What exactly inspired this piece?"

"You."

"I know, but did I do something?"

He picked up the beads and the rose gold pendant before he started to stitch it into the lace. He was quiet for so long it didn't seem like he was going to answer me. Maybe he was concentrating so hard that he hadn't heard me. Or maybe it was a question not worth answering. "Yes."

I closed his sketchbook and stared at him. "What?"

"When you threatened to tell my family the truth if I didn't treat you better." He started in one corner of the fabric and then slowly moved downward. "It annoyed me, but I respected it. It was smart, resourceful, and badass. Reminded me of something a queen would do. It made me want to fuck you even more…"

Once again, Conway Barsetti was an enigma. He wanted me to be the quiet submissive who did whatever he asked, but whenever I fought him, he seemed to respect me more. When I made demands, he argued against them but caved. It was complicated, and I still didn't understand it.

He worked for another thirty minutes, completing the piece and making a royal design. It was beautiful, magnetic. He removed the base fabric from the mannequin then sewed the pieces together. It took him four hours to complete it entirely, but once he was done, it was a wearable piece of art. He examined it with his fingertips, looking at the minor details with an experienced eye. Then he turned to me. "Put this on."

I set my robe on the table and pulled the dress over my head. It fit my measurements perfectly, from the straps over my shoulders to the tightness around my waist. I kept my panties on because he hadn't made a pair to match the dress yet. I stood in front of him, admiring the way the color complemented my skin so well.

He stared me up and down, taking in every single feature as he moved down my legs. He raised his finger and made a turning motion.

I slowly turned in a complete circle, letting him see my sides as well as my behind. I continued to turn until I was facing him again, my shoulders back and my posture perfect. I watched the intensity burn in his eyes, witnessed the arousal come to life. He stared at the cut of the top, where my tits were on display. The fabric was tight around the bust, making my tits push together and create a cleavage line without padding.

"Beautiful." He rose to his full height then wrapped his arms around my waist. His forehead pressed to mine as he explored my soft skin with his fingertips. He fingered the fabric as well as my skin underneath it. He played with the straps before he dragged two fingers down the valley of my breasts. Then he moved his hands up my stomach underneath the material, investigating every single way he could touch me.

He guided me to the couch that faced the full-length mirror. He undid his jeans and pulled them down to his thighs along with his boxers before he sat down. His long and hard cock lay against his stomach, ready for me. He wrapped his fingers around his shaft and slowly jerked himself as he held my gaze.

Seeing him touch himself immediately turned me on.

A drop formed on the crown of his cock, and he smeared

Beauty in Lingerie

it away with his thumb. "Panties off. Leave the lingerie on."

I peeled off my black thong and left it on the ground. I knew exactly what he wanted based on the way he was sitting. He wanted me to ride his cock just as I did before. He wanted to sit back and watch me enjoy him, watch me bob up and down on his length.

I straddled his hips and pointed his length at my entrance. I slowly slid down, sheathing his cock until I was sitting on his balls. His entire length was inside me, and I had to take a moment to get used to the immense stretching.

Conway gripped my ass and stared at my reflection in the mirror, seeing my back as I sat on his impressive dick. "This pussy…is incredible." He took a deep breath as he gripped my cheeks even harder. "You're always so wet for me."

I was always wet anytime I was in the same room as him. It couldn't be helped. My mind and body were at war with each other. My mind knew it was wrong, but my body couldn't care less. My pussy wanted this big cock every day, wanted to feel the stretching it finally had gotten used to. I was addicted to how good it made me feel.

"Fuck me, Muse." He dragged my hips upward then back down again, making me ride his cock.

I smeared my wetness all over his length. Up and down I moved, my clit rubbing against him at the same time. I wrapped my arms around his neck as I grinded, feeling the goodness between my legs immediately. Being on top was my favorite position because I could fuck him as hard or as slow as I wanted.

A moan emerged from deep in his throat.

I rode him harder, my face pressed to his as my thighs worked to take him over and over. I felt the burn between my legs as soon as the climax approached on the horizon. It was coming, starting in my stomach before it migrated downward. I rode him harder and harder, forgetting about how much I despised him and focusing on how amazing his dick felt. So thick and long, it hit me perfectly. I moved harder, stimulating my clit until my body couldn't take it anymore. I came with a groan, my eyes locked on to his as another wave of arousal surrounded his dick.

He dug his fingertips into my ass, and that same focused look came over his face. His features tinted red, and he was about to explode. He leaned back and held on to my hips as I did all the work. He sat back and enjoyed it, his jaw tightening as the pleasure drowned him. "Fuck…" He yanked me down so he could come with his entire length inside me. He pressed his face into my neck as his arms wrapped around me. He breathed into me then pressed a kiss against my neck.

I never wanted to be the recipient of his kiss again. Anytime I thought of his mouth, I thought of the lipstick the women left all over the collar of his shirt. I thought of the kisses they left on his earlobe and chest.

I wanted nothing to do with that.

Before he was fully soft, I got off him. I removed the

lingerie and set it on the table. He would call Nicole, and she would pick it up so the right amount of fabric could be ordered for production. My clothes were on the table where I left them, so I quickly put them back on. I could just head down to the stables and get to work, but now I wanted to wash the area between my legs and get rid of his come.

Conway remained on the couch, beautifully naked with a sleepy expression in his eyes. "No showering."

I tied my shirt together at my waist. "Excuse me?"

"No showering," he repeated. "And if you do it anyway, I'll turn off your water."

I knew exactly what he meant. He knew I was trying to wash him off me because I despised him. Of course, it was a blow to his ego, and he couldn't swallow the attack on his pride.

"You're going to work outside all day with my come inside you. That's my fantasy—and you will fulfill it."

8

Conway

I'D BEEN IN A BAD MOOD LATELY.

Every time I sat down to make a new sketch, nothing left my fingertips and appeared on the page.

I'd flat-lined.

The last pieces I made were exceptional. My ideas were flowing on to the page at an exponential rate. I was producing more work than ever before in a fraction of the time it normally took me.

I'd never felt so inspired.

But now, I'd crashed into a brick wall. My thoughts were muddled, and I couldn't picture anything. I couldn't even decide what kind of fabric would suit the new line. All I had were a few ideas I made weeks ago, but my creativity had dried up like a grape in the sun.

Fuck.

I was in the studio in Milan when Nicole walked inside. "Conway, the distributors are manufacturing The Queen on time. It should be ready to hit stores before you release your next line. If we want to keep on schedule, I need the next three pieces for the show."

What set me apart from other designers was my productivity. I always had something new for people to look forward to. Other designers reinvented the same idea over and over. They milked their products until the last drop fell. But that wasn't me. Creating something new was the best marketing strategy that could be implemented.

"Do you have them?"

"Just a few sketches."

Nicole hid her surprise, but she knew it was out of character for me to be unprepared. "Can I see?"

I opened my notebook to the first page.

She looked down at it, studying it through her thick glasses. She tilted it slightly, as if she were trying to study it at a better angle. Then she turned the page and examined the next drawing.

Her silence already told me everything.

She turned the page again and surveyed the last one.

I didn't care about anyone's opinion but my own. But right now, I knew I'd lost my touch.

She shut the book without saying anything. "If you need more time, we can postpone the next show. The date hasn't been made public, so no one would know otherwise."

She didn't like my sketches either. "Give me a few more days."

"The first two pieces are wonderful," she said. "I know those will get a lot of attention."

"Yeah…"

Nicole didn't linger much longer. She knew when she wasn't welcome. That was what I liked about her so much. She wasn't chatty, and she wasn't uncomfortable with my silence. "Let me know if you need anything." She walked out and left me alone with my thoughts.

My thoughts of self-loathing.

I knew this had something to do with Muse.

She'd stopped kissing me, and the second that connection was broken, it seemed like I'd lost her. She despised me because of the way I hurt her. She probably thought I was screwing some other woman right at that moment.

But I wasn't.

I didn't even want to.

Should I just tell her that? Come clean? Or would that lead me down a worse path?

Never in my life had I been with just a single woman. I vowed I never would be. My life was too good, my work was too important.

But now my work was suffering.

It wasn't because Muse stopped being my fantasy. It wasn't because the sex had turned stale. It was because I could feel her disgust for me. Her disappointment weighed me down like a ton of bricks. She didn't look at me the same way, with admiration and respect. Now she preferred to be on her hands and knees when we screwed so she wouldn't have to look at me.

And she wouldn't kiss me.

Not because she wouldn't allow it. She simply didn't want to.

Now she was just using me for sex, using me for casual passion. It was exactly what I wanted in the beginning.

But so much had changed.

Regardless of the decision I made, I lost. I would either make an exception for this woman and open a door to a path I'd never trod, or I would continue to let my work suffer. My fantasies and desires had changed. It went from casual passion with multiple women to the worship of one single queen.

My queen.

It was because of her that I'd released my best work. It was because of her that my career soared to new heights.

But the second she knew what she meant to me, the relationship would change. She would have power over me—a lot of power. Would she abuse it? Or would she accept that power responsibly?

I had no idea.

But it didn't seem like I had a choice anymore.

WHEN I RETURNED HOME, I showered and got ready for dinner. Muse didn't eat with me anymore because she preferred my company only for sex. Unless we were fucking, she wanted nothing to do with me.

It stung.

It used to be exactly what I wanted, but now that hollowness suffocated me.

I went to her door and knocked.

"Come in."

I stepped inside and spotted her in the living room. She was sitting on the couch in front of the TV with a book open in her lap. She'd showered after working outside all day, and now she was in a navy blue dress with her hair pulled over one shoulder. She didn't wear makeup, so she'd obviously expected to have dinner alone that night—again.

She looked up from her book, a hint of hatred in her gaze. "Yes?"

I hated that look. I hated it more than anything. We hadn't

met under the best terms, and I'd done other terrible things to her that had never received that kind of coldness. I took her virginity, controlled every aspect of her life, and used her for my own gain. But none of that crossed a line. Only when she thought I slept with someone else did it truly affect her. It pushed her away because it hurt her down to her core.

Which meant she cared about me.

And the fact that I couldn't fuck anyone else meant I cared about her.

How the hell did this happen?

When I didn't answer, she repeated herself. "Yes?"

I sat on the couch beside her and pulled the book out of her hands. I shut it and tossed it on the table. "Have dinner with me tonight."

"No, thank you." She crossed her legs and turned her gaze to the TV.

I grabbed the remote and turned it off.

She directed her irritated gaze on me. "How about we fuck, and you just leave me alone?"

I closed my eyes for a moment, feeling the insult sink all the way into my stomach. Her tone was so cold, it felt like she stabbed me with an icicle. She ripped my heart into a million pieces. Until that moment, I didn't know I had a heart. I hated the way she hated me. I despised myself for hurting her so much. I should have just been honest instead of letting her pain fester into contempt.

Or I shouldn't have allowed myself to care about her to begin with.

"You hate me that much, huh?" I whispered.

She didn't answer.

"There's something I need to tell you. I guess I'll say it now since you won't have dinner with me…"

She crossed her arms over her chest and stared straight ahead, refusing to look at me.

I sat back against the couch and watched her, seeing the seemingly invisible walls erected around her. I'd hurt a woman who'd already been hurt enough. Instead of hiding away my loyalty and commitment, I should have been real. "I haven't been with another woman since the day we met."

She slowly turned her head my way, her eyes still guarded.

"The other night, I met Carter at my lingerie club. We talked about business. He had a few women with him. He pressed one on to me, but I wasn't interested. Then he accused me of actually caring about you…so I tried to prove him wrong. I let the woman sit on my lap and kiss me. But when it came down to taking her home, I couldn't do it. And when I say I couldn't, I mean, I couldn't force myself to do something I didn't want to do. This woman was gorgeous, and I didn't feel anything. I was never hard or even attracted to her. Carter gave me shit about it, and then I drove home. All I wanted to do was come back here and be with you."

Her gaze didn't change because her guard was still up.

"I lied because I didn't want you to know how I felt. I didn't want you to know we were monogamous. I didn't want you to think I actually cared about you…that you were enough to satisfy me. Honestly, I've never been with just a single woman before. This is my first time. This is the first time I've ever wanted to bed the same woman over and over again…and never get tired of it. I don't want meaningless, passionate sex. I don't want a different woman every night. I just want you…and that fucking terrifies me."

Her breathing escalated, her small breaths growing deeper and louder. Her gaze changed, slowly softening as the words sunk in.

"I'd rather you think I'm a promiscuous ass than let you believe you mean something to me. And I would have kept up that lie if it weren't affecting my work so much. I haven't made a decent sketch in weeks. I talked to Nicole this afternoon, and she suggested we push back the next show because my work hasn't been up to my usual standard. My world is falling apart, and it's all because of you. So now I'm telling you the truth…so you can stop hating me. I hate seeing that disdain in your gaze. I hate the way you fuck me now…like it doesn't mean anything. I want it to be what it was before."

Her arms tightened across her chest, but the look she gave

me turned gentler. The hatred faded away, and she gave me a new look entirely. "The only reason you're telling me this is because it's affecting your work?"

I nodded. "I guess."

"How do I know you aren't lying to me?"

I shrugged. "I guess you don't. But I'm not. I'm far more embarrassed telling you this than sleeping with someone else…so that doesn't add up."

She looked forward again.

"Muse?" I whispered.

"What does this mean?" she whispered back. "What do you want?"

"I want what we had before…but now I'm telling you I'm committed to you. I won't be with anyone else. Just you."

"Because you care about me?"

"Yes."

"What else does it entail?"

I knew what she was really asking. "I'm not looking for romance or love. I'm not really looking for anything. All I know is, I only want to be with you. It doesn't mean I'm your boyfriend or I'll be your husband someday. It just means…that it's only the two of us. There's no one else but you and me. I don't want you to expect anything more because it won't come. But I'll be your friend, your partner, and I'll always be faithful to you. And of course, I'll be honest."

"You weren't honest before."

"I know, but I will be now."

She pulled her knees to her chest.

I was hoping for a stronger reaction than this. "I'll give you everything you want. You have my respect, my friendship, and my fidelity."

She was still quiet.

"What is it, Muse?"

"It's just taking me a second to process this."

"What is there to process?"

"I was so hurt when I thought you were with someone else…" She closed her eyes for a moment. "It's such a relief to know that you weren't…and it's taking me a second to process that feeling."

Somehow, that made me feel even worse. I scooted closer to her on the couch and wrapped my arm around her shoulders. I pulled her into me and looked down into her face, seeing her thick eyelashes curl toward the ceiling. "Why does it hurt you so much?" She enjoyed my company and my body, but I didn't suspect she loved me. After what I did to her, how could she?

"I don't know. I guess it made me feel like I wasn't good enough for you. You tell me how amazing I am, but then you look for satisfaction between another woman's legs… and then I was afraid you would give me a disease or something."

I rested my head against hers. "And that's all."

She paused for a long time. "You say you're jealous because you don't want to share me with the world…" Her hand moved to mine. "And I guess I'm jealous too. I don't want to share you with anyone."

I interlocked my fingers with hers. Hearing her admit she was jealous gave me a sense of power. It made me feel like we were equal, like we cared about each other in the same way. I was jealous any time a man looked at her, and that was the reason I hid her away from the world. She felt the same way…and that gave us a new connection.

A connection to start over.

"Can I kiss you again?"

She tilted her head up to look at me. "You want to kiss me?"

I stared at her lips, missing them since the moment they'd been taken away. I'd taken her kiss for granted, not understanding how much I needed it before it was yanked away. "Yes."

Finally, she smiled. Her eyes lit up the way they used to, and she softened into my side. "Then kiss me."

MUSE WAS ON MY BED, propped up on her elbows with her beautiful tits looking perky and delicious. Her stomach was flat and toned from working outside all the time, and her long legs stretched to the end of the bed.

I grabbed her thong with both hands and slowly pulled it down her legs, staring at her nub once it was revealed. Her pussy had never looked so beautiful. I could see the gleam from her slit, the arousal that started before I even touched her.

I wrapped her thong around my dick, letting the soft, warm fabric stimulate me more.

She opened her legs wide, beckoning to me.

If I weren't so hard up, I'd fall to my knees and devour her pussy. Right now, I wanted to devour her lips with mine. I wanted to push my dick inside her, to feel that moisture she produced all on her own.

I crawled up the bed and moved between her legs. I locked my arms behind her knees and guided her back until she was flat against the bed. Her nipples were hard, and her chest was flushed pink. I held myself on top of her and rubbed my cock between her folds. She was so wet, I could already feel it.

Her hands started at my arms, feeling my biceps and shoulders. Then she explored my chest, feeling my pectoral muscles and my chiseled abdomen. She slightly arched her back and moved, rubbing against my hard dick with her pussy.

This was exactly what I wanted. Muse writhing and panting for me. The hatred was gone from her eyes, and now she couldn't wait to have me. She didn't need lingerie tonight. In just her skin, she was the sexiest woman in the world.

And she was all mine.

I pressed my mouth to hers and kissed her, finally allowing my mouth to have what it wanted. Her kiss was sexy like always, with the perfect amount of lip and tongue. She breathed into my lungs, her hot breath making my dick twitch.

I moved my hand into her hair, and I slowly rocked into her, rubbing her clit with my thick size. I kissed her harder and deeper, feeling my entire being fall into this woman. This was exactly what I wanted, not a random screw with a few girls from a club. There was only one woman I craved, only one woman I wanted to enjoy every single night.

She was my fantasy.

I wasn't even inside her yet, and I wanted to come. I felt her take pleasure in me, felt her heart skip a beat because she enjoyed the stimulation so much. Her hands were all over me, grabbing everything and dragging her nails deep into my flesh.

I trailed my kisses to her ear and breathed in her canal. "Muse…"

She dragged her nails to my ass and yanked on me, begging me to move inside her. "Conway…please."

I pointed my dick at her entrance and slowly slid inside, feeling more lubrication than I'd ever felt in my life. I slid right in, knowing her pussy wanted me just as much I wanted her. I moaned into her ear, wanting her to listen to exactly how much I adored her. I'd never been between the legs of a more beautiful woman, a woman who made me feel more like a man. "Fuck…" I moved until I was completely sheathed, my balls hitting her ass. I'd been with her many times, but this somehow felt like the first time.

She wrapped her arms around my neck and nibbled and moaned into my ear. "Conway."

The hairs on the back of my neck stood on end, and my dick twitched inside her. Every time she said my name, I thought I might explode. It was the sexiest thing I'd ever heard. I turned my face back to hers and felt her lips with mine. She was eager for me, giving me her tongue immediately.

I started to rock into her.

The sex was slow and steady. I moved inside her, but barely. My lips were focused on hers, and my chest pressed against her luscious tits as my hips thrust inside her. My balls lightly tapped against her ass, hitting her right between the cheeks. I could feel all her cream, all the lubrication her perfect pussy produced for me. The kiss was just as good as the sex, hot and heavy. Our lips came together, broke apart, and then came together again.

I'd never wanted this, and now I wanted it more than anything. I could pick up a random woman and have good sex with no emotion, but now that felt empty. This was so much better, to feel how much this woman wanted me despite my enormous size. Her lips constantly trembled against my mouth, and her fingers yanked on my hair. She rocked back with me, wanting my dick as much as I wanted to give it to her.

She spoke against my mouth, interrupting her kisses. "I'm going to come…"

I didn't need a warning because I knew exactly when she was going to release. She squeezed my dick with an iron fist. I sucked her bottom lip and pushed into her deeper, getting my dick all the way inside.

She exploded around me a moment later, her screams deafening me. Her nails dug into the back of my neck, and her moans turned incoherent. She was a slave to her pleasure, turning into a woman who was a subject to her hormones. "Yes…Conway."

I'd missed this intense connection. I'd missed her kiss, her enthusiasm. The first time I had her, she cried during most of it. But she still came anyway, and that was the biggest turn-on ever. But now she was experienced, practicing on me until she became an expert in the sack. She knew exactly how to please me because I was the only man she'd ever fucked.

Only man.

As much as I wanted to come, I wanted this to last a long time. It felt right again, my fantasy a reality once more. It was easy to get lost in the pleasure. Time stood still, and all I could feel was the sensation erupting all over my body.

When she finished her climax, her eyes focused again, and she ran her hands up my chest. "God…that felt good." We'd been screwing every night for the past two weeks, and while she came each time, it wasn't as enjoyable. She preferred this connection too, the strong heat between us. "So fucking good."

I widened her legs more and moved into her deeper, grinding my pelvis against her throbbing clit. My warm breaths fell on her face, and I looked at the erotic gleam in her eyes. "I'm only getting started."

WE LAY side by side in the dark, both tired and satisfied from the extensive fucking we'd just done. My sheets were soaked with sweat and sex. I'd come inside her twice, so her pussy was stuffed with my seed. I felt like I'd run a marathon. I was exhausted, but I also felt like I'd achieved something great.

My inspiration had returned.

I pictured her wearing a white thong with a jewel in the center, a representation of the most beautiful gem between her legs. A push-up bra was on top, pearl white and innocent. The same jewel was in the center of the bra, right in the valley between her tits. The white represented her innocence, the jewel represented her flawless value. She was purchased for a hundred million dollars—because that was how much she was worth.

She sat up on her side of the bed then ran her fingers through her hair.

My eyes shifted to her back.

She sat there for a few seconds, staring into the darkness of my bedroom. Then she placed her feet on the floor and stood.

I sat up and leaned against the headboard. "Where are you going?"

"To bed. If I don't leave now, I'll fall asleep and never wake up."

"Then fall asleep."

She turned around and faced me, the moonlight shining through the window and highlighting her face. "You want me to stay?"

"Yes."

Instead of hopping back into bed, she continued to watch me.

I held her gaze, trying to understand her hesitance.

She finally crawled back into bed, her perfect figure highlighted by the moonlight. She got under the covers and rested her head against the pillow, her hair messy from rolling around for the last few hours.

I lay beside her then hooked her leg over my hip. I brought us close together, cuddling with her face-to-face. I'd been sleeping alone my whole life. A man like me needed the entire bed to himself. I was six three, and my muscles created constant heat that warmed the sheets. Another body nearby just made me hot. But I wanted this woman beside me, wanted her soft skin against mine. I stared into her face and watched her close her eyes. Once she drifted off, her breathing became deep and slow.

I studied her features, from the bow shape of her top lip to her slender nose. Every single feature was so perfect I wondered if she'd been created by a Greek god. She'd been molded from clay then brought to life. Never in my life had I seen a woman so stunning, so flawlessly perfect. She made me jealous because I was the only man who deserved such a perfect woman. I was the only one rich enough, powerful enough, and strong enough to bridle a woman such as her. Only a man like me had the means to protect the greatest treasure in the known world.

My hand glided up her hip to the deep curve in her waistline. I moved farther up until I felt the swell of her tit. Her skin was softer than Greek sand, and her complexion was balanced between olive and cream. A small freckle appeared once in a while, but other than that, she was completely unmarked.

I didn't judge myself for being so obsessed.

Her legs were the perfect length, every model's dream. In five-inch heels, she finally came up to my chin. Even her feet were sexy, perfectly created. I wouldn't change a single thing about her. I'd been working with models for the past decade, and not once did I ever come across a woman more beautiful.

Muse was perfect.

I was tired and satisfied, but I was more interested in watching her sleep. It didn't surprise me that Knuckles wanted her so bad. He went up to fifty million just to have her, but he knew there was no price I was unwilling to pay. I would have doubled my price just to have her.

She was mine.

I leaned in and kissed her on the mouth, giving her a slight kiss that wouldn't wake her up. Even when she didn't kiss me back, her kiss was still better than any other I had. I moved my face into her neck and brought her closer to me, making sure there was no space in between us. We were a single person, wrapped up together and intertwined.

And I liked it.

THE NEXT MORNING, I returned from my swim and stepped inside the living room in my bedroom suite. Breakfast had been set up at the table near the window—a pot of hot coffee, a vase with a single rose, and two silver platters that were covered with stainless-steel tops.

I removed my shorts and set them in the hamper and tied a towel around my waist.

Muse stepped out of the bedroom, dressed in one of my black t-shirts. Her hair was messy and pulled over one shoulder, and she still had a sleepy look in her eyes. She must have just woken up.

"Morning."

"Morning." She ran her fingers through her hair as she walked toward me, her beautiful legs moving with grace. "How was your swim?" She was so cold to me yesterday, but now everything felt the way it used to.

"Good." I circled her waist with my arms, and I kissed her.

She rose on her tiptoes to meet my kiss with her own. Her hands moved to my bare shoulders, her skin warm to the touch.

I never thought I'd like to be greeted that way, but I enjoyed it immensely. "Hungry?"

"Always."

The corner of my lip rose in a smile, and I pulled out the chair for her so she could sit. Then I moved to the other side of the table and poured myself a mug of coffee.

She removed the lid to her dish and started to devour her

egg white omelet. Her eyes were still lidded with sleepiness, but she would perk up after another fifteen minutes.

I opened the newspaper and started to read. I was barely halfway through my first article when I felt her staring at me. I shifted my gaze up to look at her. "Yes?"

"You read the paper every morning?"

"I try."

"Why?"

"I like to know what's going on in the world." I sipped my coffee.

"You just don't seem like someone who would care. You have so many emails and other things to worry about."

Work never stopped because running such a huge empire was a constant hardship. It didn't matter how many times I worked through the night, there was always something I didn't get finished. So I'd stopped trying, realizing I needed to live my life instead of attempting to do the impossible. "Ever since I can remember, my father has always read the paper at breakfast. He did it when I was young, and he still did it up until the day I moved out. My mother usually stared out the window and sipped her coffee in silence. The first day I lived on my own, that's what I did—read the paper." I closed the newspaper and set it off to the side, knowing I wouldn't have a chance to read it anyway.

"You look up to your father a lot."

"Is it that obvious?" I asked sarcastically.

"May I ask why?"

"Doesn't every son look up to his father?"

She chuckled like I made a joke. "Definitely not. Just because you're a father doesn't mean you aren't an asshole."

There were a lot of things I admired about my father. He was honest and concise. He didn't talk much, but when he did, he got his point across very well. "I started to notice the way people spoke to him when I was young. It was always with reverent respect, even a little fear. My father commands authority without words. There's something about him that makes people stand up straight. The only person who doesn't follow this pattern is my mother. She's the only one with permission to speak to him however she wants—and he allows it. But I know he allows it because he loves her. No one else will ever earn the right—not even me. He's the hardest worker I know, staying in great shape even now. He's a wealthy man who grew his fortune exponentially on his own. He earned my respect when I was a boy—and not because I had to give it to him. He raised me into the man I am now, teaching me to be a hardworking and honest man. His approval means a lot to me."

"I can tell he's proud of you."

I gave a slight nod. "When I told my parents about my ambitions, I knew it would be awkward. To tell them I design sex clothes because of my obsession with women wasn't easy. At first, my mom asked if I was gay. My father knew I wasn't because he'd caught me in my promiscuous ways…many times. He just never told her about it. They both wanted me to take over the wine business. My father wants to hand me his legacy. But when I told them this was the path I'd chosen, they both accepted it. My father said he was proud of me and has always accepted me exactly as I am. That approval means the world to me."

She smiled. "Your parents are lovely. I really like them."

"Yeah…they're great." I knew they hated the fact that I lived five hours away, along with Vanessa. If they weren't rooted in place because of their wine business, they'd probably move here to be closer to us. To my parents, family was everything. My father lived less than five miles away from his brother. The Barsettis were magnetically attached to each other.

"I hope we see them again soon."

"I'm sure we will."

Muse drank more of her coffee then cut into her omelet. She took a few more bites, her eyes downcast.

I watched her face, noting how beautiful her skin was in the morning light. When the other models removed their makeup, they looked like completely different people. Their features weren't nearly as attractive. Muse was the first woman I'd met who actually looked better without makeup.

She caught my stare and met my look. "What?"

I didn't answer her and took a bite of my breakfast.

Muse continued to stare at me, her gaze confident. She drank her coffee then cleared her throat. "I have a demand."

"A demand?" I set down my fork and tilted my head slightly. "What does that mean?"

"You lied to me and hurt me. I want something in compensation."

Judging by her change of tone, she'd been thinking about this for a while. Perhaps she'd been considering it since the moment she woke up. "Alright."

"I don't want my own room anymore. I want to live in here—with you." She held my gaze with the same confidence as before, prepared for me to challenge her. She knew she had me cornered because I had misled her for so long.

That meant she wanted to sleep with me every night. She wanted to share my space with me constantly. She wanted to be integrated into my life. Our stuff would be shared, and I would see her things on my bathroom counter every single morning. My drawers would be cleaned out to accommodate her things.

My initial reaction was to say no, but that was out of spite. I wanted to stand my ground out of principle. But I knew I needed to stop doing that. I wanted her beside me every night. I wanted sex every morning before work and every night before bed. I wanted to stare at her as much as I could, to treasure her beautiful features constantly.

I wanted all of her.

She held my gaze without blinking, still waiting for a response.

I drank my coffee and dragged out my response on purpose, making her wait for my judgment. "Okay."

Her expression immediately slackened into one of surprise. "Really?"

I nodded.

"That was a lot easier than I thought it would be…"

"May I ask why you want to live in here with me?"

She shrugged in response. "I just do."

My eyes narrowed. "I want a better answer than that, Muse."

She resisted me at first, giving me her silence. But she eventually folded under my gaze. "I sleep better next to you. I feel safe. I like your smell…your body heat. It makes me feel like less of a prisoner and more of a partner. It gives me the affection that I need, the normalcy that I crave."

I liked that answer, down to the last detail. "Anything else?"

She looked into my eyes as she spoke. "I like sleeping next to you…when your come is sitting inside me."

Good answer.

———

I DROVE to the studio in Milan with Muse in the passenger seat. I'd fucked her on my bed before we left, filled her with as much come as she could take, and then hit the road. Now she was full of me, my seed dripping into her panties.

Listening to her request to share my room with me got me so damn hard.

We arrived at the studio then stepped inside the entryway. I had to check a few things with Nicole, and when Muse asked to come along, I didn't refuse her. We reached the second landing, and I ran into a few models that were preparing for a photo shoot. They were wearing the new lingerie I had just designed and handed off to Nicole.

"Conway." Naomi moved into me, her lips ready to kiss my cheek.

Muse hooked her arm through mine and pressed her body against me, claiming her territory as publicly as possible. "We should get going, Conway." Her lips were just inches from my face, taking away any chance Naomi had to kiss me.

I could barely contain the grin that wanted to stretch across my face. "I'm sorry, ladies. I'm running late."

Muse pulled me to the stairs, and we walked up together, her arm still hooked in mine for everyone to see.

"You really are jealous," I said under my breath.

"How would you feel if a man kissed me on the cheek?" she countered.

I wouldn't like it at all. I didn't even want anyone to shake her hand. "Point taken." We walked to the third floor where my studio was and stepped inside. To my surprise, Carter was already standing there. He was in a gray suit with a black tie. Anytime he was dressed that way, he usually had a business meeting of some sort. Any other time, he was dressed in jeans and a leather jacket.

His eyes immediately went to Muse, and a grin stretched across his face. "Conway's muse. I don't think we've met." He stepped toward her and extended his hand.

She pulled her arm from my grasp and placed it in his. "Nice to meet you. You must be Carter."

He leaned in to kiss her on the cheek.

"Carter." My tone was enough to warn him to rethink his actions.

He stepped back, still grinning. "Alright. We'll do this the American way." He shook her hand. "A pleasure to meet you, Sapphire. Conway talks about you often."

"I hope he says good things," she said.

His eyes shifted to me. "Only good things."

I wanted to smack him upside the head. "Did you need something, Carter?"

"I was in this neck of the woods and wanted to see if you wanted to get lunch. Nicole told me you were in today."

"I've got a lot of work to do today, Carter. How about tomorrow?"

"My parents told me we'll be having dinner at your folks' place on Friday. We'll catch up on the drive."

No one had told me about this dinner. "Didn't realize that was happening."

"I'm sure you'll get the call soon enough. And bring your woman along. I'd love to get to know her on the drive down." He winked at me before he headed to the door. "See you soon." He walked out and left us alone.

"I'm glad I can put a face to the name now," Muse said. "You look alike."

"People think we're brothers, unfortunately."

"He seems friendly."

"He's only friendly with you because it pisses me off."

She smiled. "It only pisses you off because you get so jealous." She grinned then walked to the table, her confidence growing because she knew she put me in my place. "So dinner on Friday?"

"Apparently."

"This will be at the house where you grew up?"

"Yes."

"I'm excited to see it."

I hadn't invited her, but I didn't have much of a choice in the matter. My parents would expect me to bring her, and Vanessa would pester me until Muse was sitting beside her in the back seat.

I approached the table and opened my notebook.

"What ideas are you working on?"

"A good one came to me last night."

"Yeah?"

I flipped to the right page.

She examined my drawing as she tucked her hair behind her ear. "I like it. Simple and elegant. Most of your pieces cover more skin, but this one doesn't."

"I think the color and fabric will look perfect against your skin." I grabbed the piece of fabric from the table and returned to her. I held the soft material against her arm and admired the way it suited her skin tone. "Perfect." I set the piece of fabric on the table.

"Can I help?"

"No." I grabbed a bolt of the fabric and set it in my space on the table.

"Then what can I do?"

"Wear it when I'm finished."

"Alright." She sat on the stool by my side and stared at my hands as I worked.

Nicole walked in a few moments later. "Conway, I'm glad you're here. I need to speak to you in private."

I didn't stop what I was doing. "You can speak in front of Sapphire." She was an essential part of my life now. She knew about my work, about my routine, and she shared my bed with me. No point in keeping secrets from her.

"Conway, I must insist." Nicole stood on my right, her hand resting on the table.

Nicole wouldn't override me like that unless it was important, so I turned to Muse. "Could you step outside for a moment?"

"Of course." She stepped out and shut the door behind her.

I set down my tools then turned my full focus on Nicole. "What is it?"

"Andrew Lexington of Lady Lingerie is downstairs in the conference room."

Andrew Lexington was my biggest lingerie competitor in the world. He was based in America, and while he did great work, his designs weren't as original as mine. But he had a great grasp of marketing to the American people, and he didn't refrain from doing his production overseas to make his lingerie affordable. I was in the luxury business, so our approaches were innately different. I'd only met him once, and we didn't have much to say to each other. The fact that he flew across the world to my doorstep meant he had serious business to discuss. "What does he want?"

"This is the thing..." She kept her voice low, like someone could overhear us even though it was just the two of us in the room. "He actually came here looking for Sapphire. He said he's been trying to get a hold of her, but he says she has no known address, phone number, or family. So he came here asking to speak with her."

Instantly, my body tightened, and I felt the rage spike inside me. Another designer flew across the world because he was trying to hunt down my woman. Whatever he wanted with her, it wasn't good. He wanted her for his own gain—that was clear.

"I didn't know what to do, so I thought I would tell you first."

"You made the right decision, Nicole." I could barely keep my voice steady because I was so angry. "Show him to my office. I'll be there in fifteen minutes."

"And should I tell Sapphire?"

I didn't want her to know anything until I knew what he wanted first. "No."

I LEFT Muse in my studio and walked to my office on the other side of the building. Andrew was waiting for me, and I purposely made him wait an extra twenty minutes just to be an asshole.

Muse was mine. Not only was she my model, but she was my woman. She was the one sleeping in my bed every night, and I was the man who slept beside her. She was my property—end of story.

If Andrew thought he could have her, he was mistaken.

I stepped inside the office and saw the back of Andrew's head. His broad shoulders extended past the sides of the chair, and he continued to stare straight ahead at the windows that overlooked the city. The glass was so clean he could see his reflection—and mine.

I slowly walked past him to my desk, not stopping to greet him with a handshake.

Why should I?

I sat behind my desk and brought my hands together on the wood. I hardly used this office since my studio was my creative space. This room was for calculations and bookkeeping. Nicole did her work in here sometimes, leaving her documents out so I could see them when I had time.

I stared at him coldly, looking at a man ten years older than I was. He was in his early forties, and even though I wasn't even thirty yet, I had more success than he did. My name was much more respected. My lingerie was considered a luxury. Mistresses of powerful men wore my stuff. Only nobodies wore his shit. "How can I help you, Andrew?"

He retained his composure as well as I did. "I'm sure Nicole told you I'm looking for Sapphire."

"She mentioned it."

"And since I'm meeting with you, I guess I won't be speaking to her."

Fuck no. "You're bright."

The corner of his mouth rose in a smile. "She's one of the most difficult people to track down. I can only assume she has a fascinating story."

A story he would never know. "What do you want, Andrew?"

"We both know Sapphire stole the hearts of men and women everywhere at that show a few months ago. But I haven't seen her since—and neither has anyone else. Does that mean she's decided to retire?"

No. She just has a new job—fucking me. "She still works for me."

"Then why aren't you using your greatest weapon?"

"Trust me, I use her." I leaned forward over the desk, staring him down harder.

"Maybe she'd like to be used in other ways. I'm going to make her an offer to come work for me."

Like that would ever happen. "She's not available."

"Even if she's under contract, I can break the chains of her legal imprisonment."

Any problem could be fixed with enough money. Considering I was his biggest competitor, he needed to have leverage over me. By taking the most gorgeous model that ever stepped foot on the runway, he would definitely have serious power. I couldn't let that happen—and not just because of my business.

But because Muse was mine. "She's not going anywhere, Andrew."

"That's for her to decide."

No, it's not. "She's not available. I won't repeat myself a second time."

His eyes narrowed. "You think you can stop me from speaking to her? I know she lives here. It's only a matter of time before I corner her. And the fact that you're sabotaging a potential deal for this woman is sickening."

I owned her. It wasn't sickening at all. "She's mine, Andrew. Let it go."

"And what do you think your little star will say when I tell her that you refused to let me talk with her?"

I wasn't letting this man anywhere near her. She was stuck to me like glue every minute of the day. He couldn't get to her without going through me first. And no man could get through me. "I wouldn't waste your time, Andrew. I'm sure you have more important things to do."

9

Sapphire

Conway had been in a ticked mood ever since he'd stepped away from the studio. He returned with a clenched jaw and a furrowed brow, and he was short with me anytime I tried to talk to him. He was so angry that I stopped trying.

On the ride home, he was exactly the same. He gripped the steering wheel with one hand and kept his eyes on the road. He didn't make conversation with me, and it was obvious he was thinking about whatever had pissed him off.

"You know what I do when I'm mad?"

He sighed but didn't make a comment.

"I turn on music." The radio was never on when we were in the car. I wasn't even sure what he liked to listen to.

"I don't want to listen to music right now."

"Do you want to talk about it?"

"I want to do that even less."

I faced forward and looked out the window. "Alright then…" The day started off great then turned to shit. I was certain his mood had nothing to do with me, so I let it be. I hadn't done anything wrong, so there was no reason for him to be upset with me.

After five minutes of silence, his phone started to ring through the Bluetooth system. On the screen, the name of the person appeared.

Mama.

I couldn't help but smile when I saw the way he stored her name on his phone.

He sighed again then took the call. "Hey, Mom. How are you?" He hid his foul mood and spoke like everything was perfectly fine. If anyone else had called, he probably would have ignored the call.

"I'm great, Con. Your father and I just got home, and Lars is making dinner."

"I'm on my way home too."

"Then I won't keep you on the phone long. I just wanted to invite you to dinner this Friday. Your aunt and uncle will be there, along with Carter and Vanessa. I hope you can make it. Your father and I miss you."

My eyes softened.

"Of course, I'll be there."

"Great," she said. "Sapphire will be joining us as well?" The eagerness was obvious in her voice.

"Yes."

"Good. You guys can stay in your old bedroom."

We'd be spending the night. I hadn't expected that, but I guess it made sense since it was a five-hour drive.

"Sounds great," Conway said. "I'll talk to you then."

"Love you."

Conway acted like a macho man all the time, but I knew there was a softer version of himself underneath that bravado. He showed that side to me after I spent months yanking it out of him. And he showed it to his family much more easily. "Love you too, Mama."

The call ended.

Conway kept driving like the phone call never happened.

I wanted to tease him about it, but I decided to go easy on him. "Your old bedroom, huh? What's that like?"

"It's on the second story. My old furniture is still there. I have a private bath and a small living room."

I guess they lived in a mansion too. "Is that the room where you brought all the girls?"

"Yes." He finally looked at me. "Jealous?"

"No. But I'm prepared to wipe away their memory…"

He smiled for the first time since he fell into his sour mood. "I like the sound of that."

I CARRIED my stuff across the hall and hung up the clothes Dante had bought for me. A section of Conway's closet had been cleared so I could hang up my things. I didn't have nearly as much stuff as he did. He had more suits than I could even comprehend.

One of his top drawers had been cleared out, so I put my underwear inside along with the lingerie he'd placed in my dresser. His room was much more masculine than mine, decorated in dark tones and sharp furniture. My room was much prettier, with splashes of gold and champagne. But I still preferred his room to mine…since he was included.

Ever since he told me there hadn't been anyone else, my mood had drastically improved. Now the jealousy was gone, along with the stomach pains and the sorrow. He offered me everything I wanted, everything that could make me happy.

I finally had someone I could trust.

In a world so cruel, it was a blessing to have a friend like Conway. He was honest with me, took care of me, and he was loyal to me. He'd given me so much without asking for much in return. Without him, I would have nothing.

And I knew it.

He said he would never love me, and romance wasn't on the table, but that was okay. The connection and foundation we had were enough. It gave my life meaning, filled it with affection.

I didn't know how long this would last. Maybe one day he would get tired of me, and it would end.

But I wasn't going to think about that right now.

I finished moving my stuff over and then finally left my old bedroom for the last time. Now, this new space was mine, a space that smelled like a powerful man. Just when I'd sat on the couch, Conway walked inside with two hangers in his hand.

"What's that?" I asked.

"I had Dante pick up a few things for you to wear tomorrow." He set them over the back of the armchair then loosened his tie around his neck.

"That was nice." I picked up the first one and found a high-waisted skirt with splashes of black, red, and green. It immediately reminded me of Italian culture, of the infusion of the various colors. I looked at the next outfit, a navy blue sundress. "These are beautiful…"

"I'm glad you like them."

"Did you pick them out?"

"No. Nicole did. But I gave your measurements so they should fit you nicely."

I never pictured myself as a woman who had a man to buy her pretty things, but that was exactly what had happened. Conway supported me completely, paying a fortune to keep me safe and still lavishing me with expensive gifts. "Thank you, but you don't have to buy me anything, Conway. I have a lot of beautiful things already…" I suddenly felt guilty for taking a single penny from him.

He arched his eyebrow in confusion, but he somehow made it look sexy. "I'm aware of all the things I don't have to do. I do them because I want to. Don't ever say that to me again." He pulled his tie out of his collar and unbuttoned his shirt. "Vanessa and Conway will be here tomorrow at one. So be packed and ready by then."

"Alright."

He stripped off his clothes and dropped them on the floor as he made his way to the bathroom. Like breadcrumbs, they followed him all the way to the other side of the bedroom.

Instead of leaving them on the floor to be wrinkled, I picked them up and hung them on a hanger so Dante could collect them with the laundry. I could only guess how expensive Conway's clothes were, so I didn't want them to get ruined on the hardwood floor.

In his bedroom, his boxers had made it to the hamper. He stood naked with a towel over his shoulder. Perfectly chiseled with nothing but muscle, he was a walking fantasy. He constantly told me I was his greatest desire, but I was certain he was the desire of every woman on the planet. His appeal had nothing to do with his money or his success. It was all in his appearance—perfection.

He watched me hang up his old suit. "What are you doing?"

"I don't want your clothes to get ruined."

He gave me another look before he opened the door to the bathroom. "Shower with me."

"I already showered after the stables."

He leaned against the wall, his green eyes throbbing with annoyance. "I wasn't asking, Muse. I was telling."

I crossed my arms over my chest. "I thought we were partners now?"

"Doesn't mean I'll stop bossing you around. That's here to stay. Now get your ass inside."

"I hear shower sex is dangerous."

He grinned. "Any kind of sex with me is dangerous."

HE FOLDED me underneath him and thrust into me hard, his body working up a sweat because he'd fucked me deep right from the beginning. His ass clenched and relaxed as he rocked his hips into me, giving me his entire length over and over. The headboard tapped against the wall, and my tits shook with his movements.

My nails dug into his back as I held on, and my orgasm gripped his dick so tightly I didn't think I would ever let go. I sheathed him with my come, my screams hitting him right in the face. Missionary was my favorite position, and it seemed to be his favorite too because it was how we did it most of the time. I loved watching the intensity of his expression, the way he concentrated as his large dick rammed me over and over.

He came a moment later, his cock twitching inside me as he released. He groaned in my face, dumping all of his seed within me. I could feel him fill me, feel the weight of his come along with his warmth. Now I was used to sleeping with it between my legs every single night. I was used to seeing it drip down my legs when I got in the shower in the morning. It was a part of my life now. Conway was a part of my life.

He pulled out of me then lay beside me, the bedroom dark because we were both ready for bed. Fucking before sleep had become our routine. When his alarm went off in the morning, he usually moved on top of me again and we had a lazy quickie before we went to work. It was nice to climax before I was fully awake. He did all the work on top of me, and I just got to enjoy it.

Now, I lay beside him, the sweat from his chest smeared onto mine. I could smell his body as well as our mutual come. The bedroom smelled of sex, but now it was the scent I enjoyed most.

Our heavy breathing filled the bedroom as we both slowly glided back down and relaxed. My body was warm, and slowly the temperature dipped back to normal. Conway's body always ran at a warmer temperature, so he needed time to cool off before he cuddled me into his side.

He spoke into the darkness first. "How do you like living with me so far?"

"I really like it." I turned on my side so I could look at him. "How do you like living with me?"

"Not too bad."

"Not too bad?" I asked with a chuckle, knowing he was teasing.

"I like morning sex. Great way to wake up."

"Me too. I like sleeping with you because I imagine this is what other couples do. They make love then go to sleep in the same bed. I'm glad I get that experience."

He didn't have a comment to that.

"Are you ever going to tell me why you were so upset yesterday?"

He was quiet again. "No."

"What happened to honesty?"

"I said I would be honest with you. But I didn't say I would share every thought with you."

I let the insult wash over me without letting it cut into my skin. "But I'm your friend, Conway. You can tell me things."

"This is something I don't want to talk about it."

"Does it have something to do with me?"

He turned his head my way, his green eyes fierce. "I said I don't want to talk about it, Muse. Leave it alone."

When I sensed the anger in his tone, I finally backed off. I didn't want to go to bed upset, so I dropped the subject. "How long are we going to stay at your parents?"

"Until Saturday."

"That's a short trip."

"I have work to do. I made a few more sketches, and now I need to create them."

"What did Nicole think about them?"

"She liked them," he answered.

"Do you have a show coming up?"

"I was thinking of doing one in six weeks."

"That's pretty soon. Where would it be?"

"New York."

My hometown. I assumed I wouldn't be able to accompany him since I was a wanted fugitive in my own country. The government took tax evasion seriously. That would mean I'd have to stay here alone. The idea of not having Conway around terrified me. At that moment, I realized just how reliant I was on him, how much I needed him to feel safe. "I see. I'm guessing I won't be in the show?"

He shook his head. "Never again."

"Then I'll stay here?"

He turned on his side and faced me, our faces just inches apart. His muscular body was rigid and hard, the outline of his biceps visible even in the shadows. His hand moved under the sheets and grabbed my hip. "Why would you stay here?"

"I don't need to remind you of my list of crimes…"

"Don't worry about that. When you're with me, you're above the law."

"And him…"

Conway knew what I meant. "You never have to worry about him, alright? Stop being scared, and stop looking over your shoulder. My power constantly surrounds you— at all times." He pulled me into him, cuddling with me under the sheets. His body was like a radiator, always blowing heat. He trailed his fingers down my back, slowly feeling my soft skin over my spine. His eyes remained locked on mine, his green eyes filled with affection.

"Alright."

He rested his forehead against mine then closed his eyes. His breathing changed after a few minutes, and he slowly drifted off to sleep.

I closed my eyes and matched my breathing to his. I cherished his smell and the warmth he surrounded me with. It was easy to feel peaceful, easy to feel safe. There was something about Conway that made me feel innately comfortable. I came to this country with just the clothes on my back and without a friend to turn to, and he became my savior. He took care of me, made all my problems go away. No one else in the world would have done that for me.

No one.

VANESSA WORE a bright blue sundress with matching sandals. The color was brilliant against her olive skin and pretty eyes. No matter what she wore, she looked lovely. She had a natural beauty any woman would die for. "You're going to love my parents' house. It's been in the family for three generations now."

"Wow. I'm sure it's beautiful."

Carter and Conway helped Dante load the back of the SUV while Vanessa and I spoke in the entryway. It was a cloudless sky, and the heat caused our skin to bead with sweat. Sunglasses were pushed back over her forehead, and she wore a purse that sat across her torso.

"What happened with you and that guy?" I never got the full story because Conway and I went home. Conway wanted to keep spying on her, but I finally convinced him he needed to give his sister space. She was a grown-ass woman who didn't need a babysitter.

"A few nights of super-hot sex," she said bluntly. "But I didn't see it going anywhere. He's a nice guy, but we really don't have much in common. Our conversation ran stale, but the passion never suffered. So I got him out of my system before I moved on."

"That's too bad. At least you got something good out of it."

"Yeah. He took the rejection kinda hard, but he'll get over it."

"What did you tell him?" I asked.

"The truth. We have nothing in common, just good sex. So he suggested we keep having sex."

I chuckled. "Of course he did."

"But I told him I didn't want to get attached to him, so it was easier if we just went our separate ways. He wasn't happy about that, but he accepted it."

I liked the way Vanessa was real about everything. Nothing with her was complicated. She saw the world in black and white, and if she didn't see something working out, she just moved on. Nothing was personal with her. She also didn't settle for something unless it was absolutely what she wanted. It was another reason I respected her. "It's hard to find the perfect guy."

"It is. But don't worry, you'll find someone much better than Conway someday."

Conway walked by at that very moment and gave her a

glare. "You've been here for less than five minutes, and you're already annoying me."

"It usually doesn't take me that long," she said with a sigh. "Looks like I'm losing my touch."

I chuckled because I couldn't help it. Vanessa was the only person in the world who picked on Conway and got away with it. I didn't even give him that much shit.

Conway shifted his glare to me.

I shut my mouth quickly, hiding my smile.

Conway kept walking then picked up the last bag and took it to the car.

Carter moved to the passenger side and opened the back door. "Get in, ladies."

"Muse is sitting up front with me," Conway said as he shoved the keys into his pocket. He was in tight jeans and a green V-neck, the muscles of his arms looking veined and corded in the hot sun.

"Who?" Vanessa blurted.

Carter grinned. "It's his little pet name…"

"I mean, Sapphire," Conway quickly corrected. "She's sitting with me."

"Uh, no," Vanessa said. "I'm not sitting next to Carter for five hours."

"Hey," Carter said. "What the hell did I do to you?"

"No offense," Vanessa said quickly. "But I'd rather sit next to my friend."

Vanessa was the only friend I had, and it meant a lot to me that she viewed me in the same way. It didn't seem like she only liked me because I was dating her brother. We got along pretty well.

Conway dropped the argument. "Fine."

"But I'm not calling her Muse," Vanessa said. "What's that supposed to mean anyway?"

We piled into the SUV and buckled our safety belts.

Conway never answered her question.

Carter did. "It means he's psychotically obsessed with her."

"Since she's the only woman I've ever seen him with, I already figured that out." Vanessa leaned over the center console and immediately touched the radio, changing it to a station with pop music.

Conway swatted her hand away. "Chill out, alright?"

"I don't want to listen to your stupid rock music," Vanessa said. "You have the worst taste in music."

"No." Conway pushed her back and blocked her way with his arm. "I have the worst taste in sisters. Now sit back there and have girl talk with your friend."

Vanessa sat back and crossed her arms over her chest.

Gold earrings hung from her lobes, and they reflected the light anytime she slightly moved. "How do you put up with him?" she asked me. "Is he this bossy and intense with you?"

I hid my smile because she had no idea what kind of man her brother truly was. I could see Conway's eyes in the rearview mirror as he watched me, waiting for my response. "Yes…but in a romantic way."

WE WERE an hour away from the house. We drove through central Italy, seeing the countryside and endless wineries. There was so much beauty to the land that I couldn't process what I was seeing. No picture or photograph would do it justice.

"So, when are you guys going to have kids?" Vanessa said. "I can't wait to be an aunt."

"Vanessa." Conway's sharp tone said everything else he didn't say with words.

"It's just a question. You're telling me you didn't talk about that stuff before you moved in together?" Vanessa asked incredulously. "So when are you going to have kids?" She turned her face to me.

Conway had talked about children once before, but it was a general conversation. The idea of us having children together was never on the table. Right now, we were just two people who slept in the same bed and spent all their time together. I couldn't label us in any other way. But I had to say something to get Vanessa off the subject. "Sometime after we get married."

"And when will that be?" Vanessa asked.

"Vanessa." Conway said her name a second time, this time his tone angrier.

"What?" she asked incredulously. "I can't ask her any personal questions?"

"Not a single one," Conway snapped. "We're almost to the house, so just be quiet for the rest of the way."

Vanessa rolled her eyes. "Okay, hypothetically, how many kids would you like to have someday? You know, with any man, in general?"

This time, Conway stayed quiet.

Children probably weren't in the cards for me, even though I desperately wanted my own family. I was the last of my line, and if I didn't have children, I would always be alone. "Two. A boy and a girl."

"Me too," Vanessa said. "But I'm not appalled by the idea of having three."

"When do you want to have kids?"

"I'm not sure. I want to be done having my kids by the time I'm thirty. So I have a few years to find the right guy and settle down. Right now, all the men my age are immature. They're too focused on partying and having a good time. Real romance is just impossible right now. I think I want an older man."

"Alright, enough of that." Conway cranked up the music. It drowned us all, masking our conversation.

Vanessa rolled her eyes and leaned toward me so we could keep talking. "I really hope he doesn't stay like this forever. It's really annoying."

"I'm sure when you meet the right guy, he'll finally back off."

"I doubt he'll back off even then. Honestly, he's worse than my father. And you met my father. He's one intense man."

I chuckled. "I thought he was really nice."

"Because you're a woman. There's nothing alarming about Conway shacking up with a woman even if you guys aren't married. My brother can fuck every woman in Italy, and it wouldn't matter. But if I moved in with a guy and I wasn't married…my father would flip. It's totally sexist."

"I think the reason Conway gets away with it is because your father knows he's a good man. He would never hurt me, and he takes care of me far better than anyone else ever has. If you met an upstanding guy who loved you, I don't think your father would be that upset. I think he just wants to know you're in good hands."

"As logical as that sounds, I think you're wrong."

We arrived at the house forty-five minutes later. Just like Conway's house, it was a three-story mansion. With black gates in the front and vineyards as far as the eye could see, it was a classy Tuscan villa. Filled with olive trees, deep green grass, and lots of shade, it was one of the most beautiful homes I'd ever seen.

Conway turned down the music as he pulled into the large roundabout.

"This is where you grew up?" I asked incredulously.

"Yep," Vanessa said. "It's even more beautiful inside."

We got out of the car, and a young man came out to take our bags from the trunk.

Conway's parents walked out the front door, his father tall and handsome, and his mother beautiful in a black dress with her hair pulled back. His mother smiled when she saw all of us, and his father's expression hardened in emotion.

I noticed it anytime Mr. Barsetti stared at his son. His expression seemed to harden, but that intense look was just a mask for the love underneath. And when he looked at his daughter, he showed a different look entirely. It was much softer, much kinder. And I could see the pride he felt toward both of them.

It was humbling to watch, to witness a family love as strong as theirs. I'd never been close to my father, and my mother had a lot of issues. We weren't a happy family, not like this. Perhaps that was why Nathan went down the wrong path and got himself killed.

"Vanessa." Mr. Barsetti hugged her first, bringing her into his chest and kissing her on the forehead. "You look nice."

"Thanks, Dad. Mom got it for me."

"Makes sense," he said with a deep voice. "Your mother has great taste."

"I know." Vanessa moved to her mother next and practically jumped into her arms. I could see the closeness between them. They were friends as well as mother and daughter. They held each other with smiles on their faces.

Mr. Barsetti hugged Conway next, gripping him tightly before kissing him on the forehead. "Glad you're here."

"Me too," Conway answered. "But I'd drive ten hours to eat a meal home-cooked by Lars."

Mr. Barsetti smiled then clapped him on the back. He moved to me next, his hand moving to my elbow as he leaned in and kissed me on the cheek. "Hello, Sapphire. I'm very happy to see you."

I noticed Conway only allowed his father to kiss me on the cheek. Carter was also family, but he hadn't earned the right. "I'm happy to be here too. Your home is breathtaking. Conway said he has a lot of great memories here, and now I can see why."

"Thank you," Mr. Barsetti said. "That's very kind of you." His arm circled my waist, and he patted me on the back.

Mrs. Barsetti came next and hugged me, giving me a kiss on the cheek. "You look beautiful, Sapphire. That blue dress is perfect for you."

"Thank you," I said. "Conway got it for me."

"I'm glad my son has great taste," she said. "And not just in clothes." They moved to Carter next and greeted him with the same affection that they greeted their own kids. I watched them interact, feeling a distant pain in my chest.

I wasn't a jealous person. The only time I felt it was when I saw Conway with other women. But now I felt it in a whole new way. I was jealous of the love of this family, the way they were bonded together so deeply.

Conway circled his arm around my waist, his face pressed to mine. "What's wrong, Muse?"

"Nothing." I turned back to him and smiled.

When he didn't smile back, I knew he didn't believe me. "I'll ask again later. But you'll answer me next time."

―――

WE SAT in a large dining room that could easily accommodate fifty guests if they had a bigger table. A big window overlooked the yard, the large oak trees and the vineyards in the background. The landscape reminded me of Conway's home, and the resemblance wasn't a coincidence.

Conway had obviously had a happy childhood.

His uncle Cane and aunt Adelina were there as well. Cane bore a startling resemblance to Mr. Barsetti, the same facial features and the same build. His demeanor wasn't quite as rough as Mr. Barsetti's. He had a more playful attitude. Adelina was gorgeous just the way Conway's mother was. Even at an older age, she was still remarkably pretty. It didn't surprise me that Conway and Carter turned out to be two of the most handsome men I'd ever seen.

An older gentleman served us, bringing us a first course of salad and bread, and then the entrees. Despite his age, he still held himself upright. He moved a little slower than the average person, but he didn't seem upset to still be working.

Mrs. Barsetti caught me staring at Lars. "He's been in the family for a long time. He used to take care of Crow when he was a boy."

"Wow," I said. "So he's like family."

"No," Mr. Barsetti said. "He is family."

"We've encouraged him to retire, but he said he doesn't want to." Mrs. Barsetti held her glass of wine, her dark hair pulled back to reveal her slender neck and the necklace she wore. There was an ordinary button hanging from the chain. "Says without a purpose he would be lost. But we hired a few extra people to give him a hand. Now he takes a midday nap and goes to bed immediately after dinner."

"Does he live here?" I asked.

"Yes," she said. "He has his own bedroom on the bottom floor. My husband and I are on the third floor, so he pretty much has the house to himself."

Being a butler sounded like a pretty good gig. But I assumed if Lars lived at the house, he didn't have a family of his own to go to. Maybe he didn't have children either. The fact that the Barsettis had adopted this old man only made me love them more. They were the family that Lars needed to have. Now I knew where Conway inherited his compassion—from his parents.

"How do you like Dante?" Mrs. Barsetti asked.

"He's an exceptional chef," I said. "But when I first moved in, he didn't like me."

"He didn't?" Mr. Barsetti asked. "How could he not?"

"She's not explaining the whole story." Conway sat beside me, holding his utensils without cutting into his chicken. "When she first moved in with me, she didn't understand how to be waited on. So she would try to make her own lunch and do her own laundry."

"So?" I asked. "I felt bad having this man do stuff for me when I'm capable of doing it myself."

Mrs. Barsetti smiled. "You remind me of myself. I did the same thing when I first moved in with Crow."

"But she has a good point," Vanessa said. "It's strange to have someone do stuff for you. It makes you lazy. I didn't learn how to make a sandwich until I went to university. I didn't even know how to do my own laundry. That first week was rough…"

Mrs. Barsetti chuckled. "At least you learned." She turned her gaze on her son, her look innately soft. "How's work been, Con?"

Just as he did when he was at home, he used perfect table manners. He held himself perfectly straight, his elbows off the table and his movements silent. "Never better. I'm getting ready for a new product line in a few weeks."

"That's nice," Mrs. Barsetti said. "You did such a great job last time that it must be stressful to attempt to top it."

"I'm sure you can do it," Mr. Barsetti said confidently.

Knowing their son made lingerie must be awkward, but they were so supportive about it. It was obvious Conway's parents would love him no matter what he decided to commit his life to. They were the kind of parents that only existed in stories, not real life. Mr. Barsetti was obviously traditional, producing goods from the soil and selling them for profit. I didn't know much about Italian culture, but they seemed to be shining examples of it.

"How's the car business?" Cane asked Carter.

I didn't know anything about Carter, other than the fact that he was Conway's cousin.

"Never better," Carter answered. "People always want European engineering. Can't say I blame them."

"You sell cars?" I asked, genuinely interested.

"Yes," Carter answered. "But I also design them. I'm the founder and CEO of Steel Automobiles, luxury cars similar to Ferraris and Lamborghinis. They're popular across Europe, but they're increasing in popularity in the States. I started with one idea when I was seventeen and grew it into a company."

"Wow…are all the Barsettis this accomplished?" I asked with a chuckle.

"Not me," Vanessa said bluntly. "I never sign up for morning classes because I like to sleep until nine every day."

Conway moved his hand to my thigh under the table. "My sister is the black sheep of the family…"

"Just because you sleep in doesn't mean you're unaccomplished," Mr. Barsetti said. "You just do your best work at night. That's all."

Vanessa locked her gaze on to mine then rolled her eyes.

I stopped myself from chuckling.

The conversation continued, and they talked about the wine business mostly. Mr. Barsetti and Cane worked together to manage the company, and it seemed like Adelina helped once in a while. Mrs. Barsetti was a lot more involved.

"What do you do in your spare time?" Mrs. Barsetti asked me. "Do you have any hobbies?"

"I work in the stables every day," I answered. "I help

Marco clean the stalls, groom the horses, and take care of the feed and the hay. The barn requires a lot of work too. We've been having a bit of a heat wave, so we've been moving the horses inside so they stay cool."

"You work out there all day?" Mrs. Barsetti asked incredulously.

Her disappointed look made me regret telling the truth. Maybe they thought I was classless for working outside all day. Maybe they thought I should help Conway more. "Uh...yeah. I've always like horses."

Mrs. Barsetti turned her fierce gaze on Conway. "You let her do hard labor in hundred-degree weather?"

"I tried to talk her out of it, but she likes it," Conway answered. "She enjoys it. And according to Marco, she's a natural. The horses like her, and the stables have never looked better."

"I thought something was different when I stopped by," Mr. Barsetti said. "That's impressive. Good for you, Sapphire." He turned to his wife. "I thought you would admire her for that."

"I do," Mrs. Barsetti said. "I just wanted to make sure she liked it..." She finally tore her accusatory look away from her son.

Now I knew why Conway wanted to keep the truth of our relationship a secret. I could picture Mrs. Barsetti doing more than just giving him a dirty look. If she knew he bought me to keep me as property, I couldn't even imagine what she might do.

"She also helps me with my work," Conway said. "She helps me create my pieces."

"And inspires them," Carter jabbed with a smile.

Conway didn't show the slightest hint of shame. "Yes. She's my biggest inspiration." He held Carter's gaze without flinching.

The rest of his family kept eating, ignoring the incredibly awkward thing Conway had just said.

Vanessa was the only one to comment on it. "And off to the next subject…"

WE SPENT the evening on the patio, drinking wine and enjoying the assorted cakes that Lars had made. White lights were hung in the trees, and the moths floated toward the brightness. The sun had been gone for hours, but the heat still filtered across the land. I could feel it through my skin and directly to my bone.

Conway rested his arm over the back of my chair, looking handsome in his t-shirt and jeans. He had a strong chest and even stronger shoulders. It was the Barsetti build, because all the other men seemed to have a similar musculature.

He looked down at me as I ate my chocolate cake. "Like it?"

"Uh, duh. This is amazing." I kept shoveling the chocolate into my mouth, enjoying the moist cake and creamy frosting.

Conway never ate sweets. He didn't even take cream in his coffee. "There's nothing Lars can't do, not even in his eighties."

"He's eighty?" I asked incredulously.

"Eighty-five," he answered. "I can't believe it either."

"Well, he sure knows how to bake a cake." I set the plate of half-eaten cake on the table and cut myself off. "If I eat anymore, I won't be able to fit into my clothes anymore."

He chuckled. "You can eat whatever you want. You look beautiful no matter what."

I looked up at him with a skeptical look, surprised he would say something so sweet. He had a strict preference when it came to the models that wore his lingerie. I thought if I gained even a pound, I would be criticized for it. "I thought I had to stay a certain size."

"You aren't on the runway anymore. You can do whatever you want."

"Watch what you say…I'll go on an eating spree and never stop."

He pressed his face close to mine, not caring about the look his surrounding family gave us. "Go ahead, Muse."

He rubbed his nose against mine. "I'll still want to fuck you just the same." He kept his voice at a whisper so no one would overhear his words. Then he pulled away and took another drink of his wine.

Vanessa was watching us from across the table. "Mom, Dad, you know what Conway calls Sapphire?"

Mrs. Barsetti swirled her wine before she took a drink. "What?"

"Muse," Vanessa said. "I heard him say it before we got in the car."

I felt my cheeks redden instantly because the nickname was so intimate. He'd started calling me that when we first met. I'd only heard him say my birth name once or twice. To others, it might just be a nickname. But that was the name he whispered when he was between my legs. It was the name he said when he commanded me to please him. It was the name he used to possess me.

Mr. Barsetti shifted his gaze to his son and studied him with a reserved expression. His thoughts were nearly impossible to see because he hid them behind a calculated gaze. He never smiled. When he greeted his kids, he showed them affection. But a smile never broke across his lips.

Mrs. Barsetti gave him an entirely different look. It was soft, touched with a hint of a smile.

Just like the last time he was put on the spot, Conway didn't squirm. There was nothing that anyone could say to make him uncomfortable in his own skin. He knew exactly who he was, and he wasn't ashamed of that truth. He was a lingerie designer—and I was his ultimate inspiration. "Yes, she's my obsession." He brought my hand to his lips and kissed the back of my knuckles.

Now I couldn't stop the smile from spreading across my lips. I couldn't stop my eyes from softening. The second his warm lips touched my skin, I felt a shiver run down my spine. As with any other time he touched me, my body came to life. Even in front of his family, the feeling couldn't be restrained.

Mrs. Barsetti leaned toward her husband then whispered something in this ear.

His expression still didn't change.

Vanessa rose from her chair, carrying her glass of wine. "Well, I like you better when your obsession is around. So you better keep her, Con."

He held my hand on his thigh and squeezed it. "I will."

VANESSA and I sat at the edge of the pool with our feet dangling in the water. We shared a bottle of red wine and listened to the crickets chirp into the night. The stars were bright overhead because the lights from Florence were too far away. It was such a peaceful place, reminding me of the home I shared with Conway.

"My parents got married under that tree." Vanessa

pointed to a mighty oak tree away from the patio. "At least, that's what I've been told."

"That's nice."

"It was a small wedding with just a few people." She pointed to a different tree. "We used to have a tire swing that hung from that branch, but a bad storm came through and snapped it off the trunk. We never got another one."

"I wonder what Conway looked like as a boy."

"There's pictures all over the house. You'll see them." She kept drinking, on her sixth or seventh glass, but she didn't seem affected by the alcohol.

"You guys really know how to carry your liquor. I used to be a bartender, and so many people tip over after a few drinks."

"The Barsettis were made to drink," she said with a laugh. "I've seen my father drink wine for breakfast. He usually drinks scotch in the evenings. I'm not a fan of it. Wine has so much more flavor."

I remembered Conway mentioning that. "Conway drinks scotch too."

"Yeah, he's a younger version of my father. Sometimes I get them confused from behind."

I saw a lot of the same qualities among all of the men. Mr. Barsetti seemed to be the silent patriarch of the entire family. He ruled quietly, but his power was felt. The way Conway described him was dead on.

Vanessa turned to me, her dress pulled up to her thighs so it wouldn't get wet. "My brother is so head over heels for you. It grosses me out, but it's so cute that it cancels out the nausea. I'm really glad he's finally found the woman to spend his life with. You know, I was afraid he'd be into some stuck-up, hoity-toity, high-maintenance, dumb bitch model type, and I'm so glad he's not. I guess my brother has better judgment than he lets on."

It was a flattering thing to say. Vanessa just gave me her approval to spend my life with her brother. Too bad it was all a lie. "We aren't getting married, Vanessa. The relationship is still relatively new…"

"it doesn't matter how long it's been. I've never been in love, but I know it doesn't work on a timetable. Whether it's been a week or a hundred weeks, it doesn't change the intensity of emotions. I don't know much about love, personally, but I recognize it when I see it. I see it when Conway looks at you. It's the same way my father looks at my mother."

Another jolt of warmth filled my insides. I knew I was his possession, his lustful obsession. He promised to give me all of him, to be faithful to me since I was the only woman he wanted. It was a commitment, but not necessarily a relationship. What Vanessa saw was our connection, the physical infatuation we had for one another. The symptoms were so similar to love that it was easy to mistake them. Since I couldn't correct her, I didn't. "Conway is a good man. I'm very lucky." I felt the sincerity throb in my heart when I said those words. If someone judged him in black and white, they'd see him as a terrible person. But when you really examined his actions in our context, he was full of goodness. He took care of me better than any other man ever could. I was nothing without him.

"Yeah, he's not so bad," she whispered. "You know, when he's not stalking my dates or prying into my personal life."

I chuckled. "Yeah, he's a little extreme."

"And he's worse with you. You probably can't even go to the store without him watching you."

She was absolutely right, but for many different reasons.

10

Conway

I sat with my father on the patio while Uncle Cane, Aunt Adelina, Mom, and Carter talked on the other side of the table. They talked about cars most of the time, but then the subject changed to his personal life.

Carter didn't have much of a personal life. It was all fucking and drinking, but of course, you couldn't tell your family that.

Muse and Vanessa sat with their feet in the pool, sharing a bottle of wine and laughing together—probably at my expense. Vanessa was probably telling Muse every embarrassing story she could think of, and Muse would tease me about it once we were alone together.

My father was quiet, drinking his wine without making conversation. His eyes were trained on the girls in the pool, watching their movements like he might miss something. His silence was suffocating. It was obvious he was thinking something, but what, no one could figure out.

Well, except my mother.

He finished his wine then refilled his glass. "They get along really well."

"Unfortunately. Vanessa has made Muse…Sapphire her new best friend." Muse was the only name I ever used, and it was difficult for me to separate the names when I was around other people. My father called my mother Button, but to this day, I had no idea why. Every time I asked, he wouldn't answer.

"Vanessa is friendly, but picky. She wouldn't be friends with Sapphire if she didn't genuinely like her."

There was so much to like about my muse. She was easy to talk to, understanding, and she had carefully crafted responses when prompted. She was as smart as she was beautiful, but she was exceptionally humble. Her appearance didn't mean much to her. She cared more about getting her hands dirty in the stables than lying by the pool all day in a bikini. "There's very little to dislike about Sapphire…if there's anything at all." I drank my wine, an aged red that my father had pulled from his cellars underneath the house.

"You seem infatuated with her." My father had never said anything like that to me before. When it came to my personal life, he never crossed that line. I'd been a man for ten years, and not once had it come up.

"Because I am."

He continued to stare at the girls by the pool. "I respect her for working in the stables. She wants to contribute to your estate. She's not just with you for your money, that's clear."

She was with me because I bought her. But if I said that to my father, he'd put me in a hospital bed. "She doesn't like to sit around. She gets bored."

"But working outside is tough work, let alone in the stables. She could cook or clean, but she decided to do something else. That woman is made of something stronger than everyone else. I can tell just by looking at her. She's a survivor, she's a hard worker. She's the kind of woman that makes a boy a man."

She definitely made me into a man every night. And she'd definitely survived horrendous tragedies. Anyone else would have been too scared to run from Knuckles in the first place, for fear of a crueler punishment. But not Muse. She hauled ass and didn't give up. She made sacrifices in order to keep going, and even when she hit rock bottom, she still kept her dignity. People earned respect when they were at the height of their success, but respect should be earned when you're at the bottom of your resources. That was when character was truly tested. Her character had been tested, and she bloomed like a rose. "Yes, she's exceptional."

"When are you going to ask her?"

"Ask her what?"

My father turned his gaze on me. "To marry you."

I held his gaze and felt my heart pound in my chest. When my father stared at me with those powerful eyes, I couldn't back down. I had to be worthy of his look. "It's too soon for that."

"But it's not too soon for her to live with you?" he countered. "If you love her, marry her."

"I never said I loved her."

"Are you saying you don't?" He narrowed his eyes.

I didn't want to lie to my father. It made me feel like shit on the bottom of his shoe. I respected him too much to give him false information. It made me feel deceitful, like I was betraying him. But to tell him the truth would be worse, that she was merely a slave I purchased for my own pleasure. I would be no better than the men he despised. His disappointment would kill me, and I would never recover from the deadly blow. "I do." I forced the words out, feeling them burn my throat on the way out. My heart rate picked up slightly, the blood pounding in my ears. An adrenaline rush moved through me, and I wasn't sure if it was from the lie I just told, or the feeling I got from saying the words. "I'm just not ready for that kind of commitment right now."

He continued to stare at me, his jaw hard and his eyes deadly.

"What?"

"I didn't say anything."

"But you're looking at me like you're saying something."

He looked forward again and gave a slight nod toward Muse. "I just know women like that are rare. Not only is she beautiful, but she's got spunk. She reminds me of your mother. And I wished I had married her sooner only so I could enjoy as much time with her as possible. A single lifetime just isn't long enough." He rested his arms on the armrests. "I tried to remain uncommitted as long as I could, but then your mother left me."

This was brand-new information to me. The limited information I had about them suggested they'd been happily in love since the day they met. "She left you?"

"Yes. She said she loved me, and I refused to say it back. I wasn't a man at the time. I was scared of feeling anything, scared of losing someone else I cared about. It was easier just to live an empty life. But when she left…I never felt more alone. Just don't make the same mistake I did. If you've found the woman you love, don't drag your feet. Be the man that she deserves. Because before you know it…" He snapped his fingers. "Someone else can replace you."

The idea of Muse being with another man besides me made me sick to my stomach.

"That's my advice, son. I can tell you're her whole world."

My father was never wrong about anything, but this was a one-time exception. Muse was jealous and didn't want to share me with anyone, but that didn't mean she loved me. How could she love me after what I did to her? How could she love me in our situation? I wasn't sure what we had, but it was a complicated relationship based on forced servitude and a strange friendship.

"I can read people well," he continued. "And I know I'm not wrong about her."

IT WAS midnight when we finally went to my bedroom on the second floor. My old bedroom was exactly how I left it, the gray comforter blending in with the dark wood of the headboard. I had a small sitting area with a TV, along with a private bathroom. It had a balcony that faced the east side of the property.

Muse stepped inside and took a look around. It was bare, tidy, and neat. I didn't have posters on the wall or collections. I'd spent most of my time outside the house when I was growing up, except at night when I'd sneak women over. That's when my obsession with lingerie emerged. Touching their bras and panties and peeling them off was the best part about sex.

She stopped in front of the bed then faced me.

"So, what do you think?"

"Of your room?" she asked.

"Yeah."

"It's nice." She peeled off her dress then unclasped her bra, keeping her gaze on me as she undressed herself. She kept her black thong on, the dark color looking incredible against her skin. Her brown curls settled past her shoulders, and she stared at me with those brilliant eyes that made my dick rock-hard.

"Still going to erase my memory of every woman I've had up here?"

"Yes." She touched my body and pulled my shirt over my head. Once my chest was bare, she moved into me and kissed me everywhere, starting at my collarbone and exploring my pecs. She moved farther down, her kiss touching my sternum and then my stomach. Lower and lower she went, her tongue tasting my hot skin.

Then she got to her knees.

Right in front of me.

She undid my jeans and yanked them down along with my boxers. My long cock popped out, already drooling at the tip. She pressed her mouth to my balls and started to kiss and suck, her warm breath drifting across my tender skin.

I definitely wasn't thinking about any of the others now. I never thought I would have a woman like her in my bedroom, all curves and beauty. I never thought such a sexy woman would rub her tongue all over my dick.

She brought my cock into her mouth and started to deepthroat him, sucking him better than last time because she had more practice. She moved her head back and forth, taking in my length over and over as her saliva dripped to her chin. She gripped my base and started to jerk me, giving me a deadly combo that made me want to explode right then and there.

Just when I hit my threshold, she pulled away.

On purpose.

My eyes narrowed as she stood up, looking sexy in that skintight thong. She pressed her hand into my chest and guided me back to the bed, a teasing look in her eyes. She shoved me, making me fall back onto the bed.

Then she crawled on top of me and straddled my hips. She moved with confidence rather than shyness. Her experience had given her new self-esteem. Now she was sexy and authoritative. She'd fucked me enough times to know what she wanted—and to know exactly what I wanted.

She rested her hands against my chest then slid down my cock, taking me in by guiding herself backward onto my length. She slowly pushed him inside until he was completely sheathed, her ass sitting on my balls.

Fuck yeah.

She pushed against my chest as she moved, using her hips to rock back and take in my length over and over. She moved slowly, making sure the bed didn't creak and the headboard didn't tap against the wall. But the slower she moved, the more I wanted to come. Her tits were beautiful in my face, and my cock was smeared with her overwhelming arousal.

She wanted to fuck me harder than I wanted to fuck her.

I propped myself on my elbows to get a better view. I sat back and watched her fuck me, watched her please herself with my body. When her tits were in my face, I snuck a kiss to each one. Her nipples were delicious, especially when they were hard like that.

She kept going, her pants and moans growing deeper.

I watched her with infatuation, watched her be the biggest turn-on ever. There was nothing I loved more than taking charge and fucking her the way I wanted. But after watching this performance, I wasn't so sure.

Seeing her want me was the sexiest thing ever.

She wanted me to think only of her, not the cherries I'd popped on this bed. She wanted me to only think about her pussy, no one else's.

I closed my eyes and resisted the urge to come. It was getting stronger by the second.

"I'm almost there."

I opened my eyes and grabbed her hips. I guided her body differently, teaching her how to rub her clit against my body on the way down before she pulled up again.

When she moaned between her teeth, I knew she recognized the difference.

I clenched my jaw as I fought the heat in my balls. My cock was already thickening, ready to fill her tight pussy with all my come. I was ready to explode, to fill my woman with everything that I had.

"God…" Her hips started to buck against me automatically once she reached her trigger. Her breathing escalated, and she hid her moans behind her teeth. She did her best to be silent as she came, but the quiet screams escaped.

I didn't give a fuck if anyone heard us. I lay back and gripped her hips, releasing inside her with a deep groan. My cock twitched happily, and I dumped all my come inside my woman. The climax was strong enough to make my chest ache, to make my balls tighten against my body.

So fucking good.

She lay on top of me and kissed me, gave me her tongue as my cock softened inside her cunt. She moved her hands into my hair and kissed me with more passion than she ever had. Her lips moved against mine with purpose, her tongue danced with mine. She moaned into my mouth like my kisses were as good as sex.

I squeezed her thighs and kissed her back.

She spoke against my mouth. "Again."

I smiled in between our kisses, feeling the intensity of her attraction. "Alright. Again."

WE HAD breakfast on the terrace again, but this time, it was just my parents and Vanessa. Carter was spending time with his parents at their place. Muse needed more time getting ready, so I headed down before her so I could enjoy my coffee.

My parents were already there, sitting under the Tuscan sun just as they did when I was growing up. Vanessa was dressed for a photo shoot even though it was just a Saturday morning with her family.

"How'd you sleep?" my mother asked.

After I let Muse have her way with me twice, pretty damn well. My childhood bed was as comfortable as ever. Now her scent was on the sheets and in the room, giving it a womanly touch that hadn't been there before.

Because only girls had been there.

"Good," I answered. "How about you guys?"

"I always sleep well," Mom answered. "With your father beside me every night."

My father was as stern as ever, not reciprocating her words with noticeable affection.

Vanessa stuck out her tongue in disgust.

Mom swatted her wrist. "When you bring your husband home, you want me to make that face at you?"

"If I talk like that, please," Vanessa countered.

"Did Sapphire sleep alright?" Mom asked.

"Yeah, she's just finishing getting ready," I answered. She wanted to do her hair and makeup perfectly for my parents. When it was just the two of us, she didn't care about her appearance. But now, she actually wanted to make a good impression. I wasn't worried about her telling my family my secret anymore. Hadn't crossed my mind once.

"Maybe you two should stay for another night," Mom said. "Take her down to the winery and show her around."

As much as I'd like to stay, I had a lot of preparations to complete. "I would, but I have too much work to do. But once this show is over, I'll take a vacation and stay down here for a while."

Mom smiled at that comment. "That sounds nice. I would like to get to spend more time with both of you."

My parents did their best not to be clingy with me, but I noticed the pain in their eyes every time I left. If they had it their way, I would be down the road from them just the way Cane was. Maybe one day it could be that way. But for now, it was too difficult. "We'd like that too."

Muse came down a moment later, looking beautiful in her new skirt and a drapey top with a floppy hat to keep the sun out of her face.

I stood up and pulled out her chair for her.

She hesitated slightly at my politeness since I didn't do this when it was just the two of us.

I leaned down and kissed her on the lips. "You look beautiful."

She kissed me back quickly, self-conscious with my parents sitting there. But she smiled anyway. "Thank you."

I scooted in her chair then sat beside her.

Vanessa stared at me in shock.

"What?" I asked with a glare.

"I just didn't know you were capable of being a gentleman," Vanessa said. "That's all…"

Mom chuckled before she drank her coffee.

My father acted like he hadn't heard her. He tuned out the heated conversations between my sister and me. All he had to do was say a single word, and it would silence the argument immediately.

We enjoyed breakfast and made small talk about the weather and the vineyards. My hand rested on Muse's thigh because it was impossible for me to sit beside her without touching her. Muse ate everything on her plate and helped herself to the bread on the table. She ate a lot more that morning than she ever did a home, clearly comfortable around my parents and in a good mood.

I liked to watch her eat. The girls at the studio drank hot water for breakfast and ate a simple slice of salmon for lunch. Their lives revolved around starving themselves and working out. I understood that was how it had to be, but I didn't want Muse to have those eating habits. I wanted her to eat like a real person. I wanted her to be strong and healthy. She wasn't on the runway, so her weight didn't matter. When she was in my bed, she could be any weight she wanted to be.

After we finished our long breakfast, we said goodbye at the gate.

Mom hugged me for a long time, like she wouldn't see me for months instead of weeks. "I love you, son." She came up to my chest, so she rested her face against my pectoral.

I patted her back. "Love you too, Mama."

She squeezed me before she finally let go. "I'm so proud of the man you've become."

My eyes softened as I looked down at my mother. "Thanks, Mom."

"You're so successful, so handsome, and you treat Sapphire so well. That's all your father and I ever really wanted… for you to be a good man."

Instead of making me feel good, shards of ice pierced me everywhere. She was flattering me, but she somehow cut me down and made me feel like shit. My mother was praising me because she thought I was a good person. But I was anything but good. Muse was with me because she had no other choice. I bought her like livestock and made her sleep with me as part of her debt.

If my mother knew, she would never forgive me.

I didn't know what to say to her, so I said nothing at all.

My father came next and hugged me. "Love you, son."

"Love you too, Father."

He kissed me on the forehead then faced me head on. "Something on your mind?"

He could read my expressions because they were nearly identical to his. "Yeah, I just remembered something I have to do at the office."

My father didn't question it. "Get home safely."

"I will."

He kissed Muse goodbye before he finally let us go.

We piled into the SUV then went to Carter's place to pick him up. My eyes were on the road, and I searched for the right street where I should turn, but I couldn't get my mother's words out of my head.

I'm so proud of the man you've become.

I wasn't a man at all.

I was a monster.

11

Sapphire

Conway dropped off Vanessa at her apartment in Milan after we'd dropped Carter at his. He got her bags out of the back and carried them inside.

Vanessa and I hugged at the sidewalk.

"My family loves you," she said. "So, thanks for putting up with Conway. I'd rather hang out with you instead of him any day."

I knew she was joking, so I smiled. "Thanks for being so good to me."

"You want to get lunch this week?" Vanessa asked. "There's this great little café right down the street you'll love."

Conway walked up at that moment.

"Yeah, sure," I said. "After a few hours at the studio, I'll come by."

"Come by where?" Conway asked, sticking his nose where it didn't belong.

"We're having lunch together this week," Vanessa said. "And, no, you aren't invited." She flipped her hair and walked off.

Conway growled quietly under his breath, annoyed with his sister.

Then Vanessa ran back and darted into his side, nearly tackling him as she hugged his waist. "You know I love you."

With the snap of a finger, Conway's anger was gone. He looked down at her before he patted her on the back. "Sometimes I forget. But I love you too."

She turned and walked back into her apartment. She waved from the doorstep before she walked inside.

I grinned at Conway.

"What?" he asked, turning serious again.

"Nothing." I climbed back into the car, and then we were on the road a moment later.

Conway drove with one hand on the wheel, and even though no one else was in the car to witness, he reached for my hand. He held it on the center console between us, his eyes on the road like the affection was completely normal. He kissed me and touched me, but those embraces always led to sex.

But this…this was something else.

"No one can see us, Conway."

His thumb gently brushed over my knuckles. "I know."

I stared at the side of his handsome face, his hard jaw and corded neck. He wore his sunglasses, and even though his pretty eyes were hidden, he still looked phenomenally handsome. Sometimes it was hard to believe that the sexiest billionaire in Italy was mine—and he paid a fortune just to have me.

"Are you going to tell me what was bothering you yesterday?"

I was hoping the subject had been forgotten. "It's stupid, and you aren't going to want to hear about it."

"It probably is stupid. Doesn't mean I don't care."

"Wow, so sweet and rude at the same time."

He grinned, showing all of his perfectly straight teeth. "Muse, tell me."

"Alright…your family is so amazing that it makes me a little sad."

"Sad, how?"

"You're just so close. Your parents love you. They love Vanessa. I don't know…you have such a beautiful gift. Even when my family was alive, we were never close. When I see the closeness and the love…I get jealous. And not jealous like I am when I see you with another woman. Jealous in a different way."

He squeezed my hand. "You feel alone."

"Yeah…"

"You're in a different country, and you've been through a lot. Makes sense. But you're forgetting something."

No, I wasn't forgetting anything. I didn't have a penny to my name, and I'd been sold in the Underground because I couldn't survive on my own for more than a day. I'd gotten myself into a shitty situation, and there was no way to get out of it. "What am I forgetting?"

"Me." He brought my hand to his lips and kissed it. "You forgetting that you have me."

WHEN WE RETURNED HOME, our bags were carried to our bedroom on the third floor, and Conway immediately went to his office to catch up on the emails he'd missed from Nicole. It was too late in the day for me to go to the stables, so I sat in the living room in his suite and turned on the TV.

My phone was on the table. I didn't have anything in it except Vanessa's number. I didn't even have Conway's number. There wasn't any point when he was constantly at my side.

But then it started to ring.

A number I didn't recognize popped up on the screen. I had no idea what the area code was here, so it wasn't clear if it was even local. I considered just ignoring it, but then my curiosity got the best of me.

I answered. "Hello?"

"Is this Miss Sapphire?" A masculine voice erupted on the other line, a voice I didn't recognize. He sounded older than me, maybe in his late thirties.

"This is she. Who's this?"

"Andrew Lexington of Lady Lingerie."

His name was vaguely familiar, but I recognized the brand right away. It was a lingerie store found in every single mall in America. You'd have to live under a rock not to recognize it. "Oh?"

"I'm the owner and designer of Lady Lingerie. It's nice to meet you, Sapphire. Tracking you down was quite an ordeal."

"And why are you trying to track me down?" I was immobilized, unsure if I should hang up, run to Conway, or keep talking.

"I'd like to make you an offer. I've contacted Conway Barsetti about this before, but he refused to allow me to see you. Not that I judge him for it. It makes sense that he's protective of you…since you're living with him."

He obviously did his research. "I have a strict contract with Conway, so whatever your offer is, I think it would be pointless. I'm flattered you want to talk with me, but—"

"Please listen to me before you shut me down right away.

Conway Barsetti is a very powerful man, but so am I. There's no amount of money I'm not willing to pay for you."

My anger rose. "I'm not a piece of livestock."

"And I'm not assuming that you are," he countered calmly. "But you should know you have options. I'm willing to double whatever Conway is paying you."

If only he knew how much he paid for me. "You can't afford me."

"Like I said, there's no amount I'm not willing to pay. Meet with me in person to talk it over."

The idea of meeting this man to talk about taking a job felt deceitful. Conway took care of me. It would be wrong of me to meet with him. "I can't. But thank you for calling, Mr. Lexington."

"Whoa, hold on. If we have to do this over the phone, so be it. What is he paying you?"

I shouldn't even tell him. "A hundred million."

Silence echoed back at me.

But that silence didn't last long. "Is that the amount of your entire contract?"

"Yes." Told you you couldn't afford me.

"I'll pay you double."

I nearly choked on my own breath when I heard what he said. "What?"

"I'll pay you double," he repeated. "For a ten-year contract with my lingerie company. You model for me, and then you can retire handsomely at the end of your run. You can buy yourself out of his contract and still have plenty left over."

That would give me enough to pay Conway back for buying me. And it would be enough to settle my debts with Knuckles, along with the money I owed in New York. I could clear my name completely.

And I could go home.

"Sapphire?"

My mind drifted away. "I'm still here."

"Does that mean we have a deal?"

It would be stupid not to take it. I could pay back Conway and not feel any guilt, and I could get everything I wanted. But something held me back. A rock formed in the pit of my stomach, and the guilt started to swell up inside me. "I…I need to think about it."

"Alright. I'll give you a call back in a week. How does that sound?"

"Yes…that would be good."

"Goodbye, Sapphire. I'll talk with you soon."

I hung up then set the phone on the table. I stared at the screen until it turned black. The conversation replayed in my mind, and I felt the weight sit on my shoulders. My weekends were spent at his parents' house, and now I was sitting there with a two-hundred-million-dollar offer on the table.

Anyone else would take it.

But I couldn't.

I didn't owe Conway anything but money. And if I paid him back, then I wouldn't have to feel any guilt. I could be free once more. But I still didn't jump on the opportunity.

Because I wasn't sure if I wanted to leave Conway…at any price.

Also by Penelope Sky

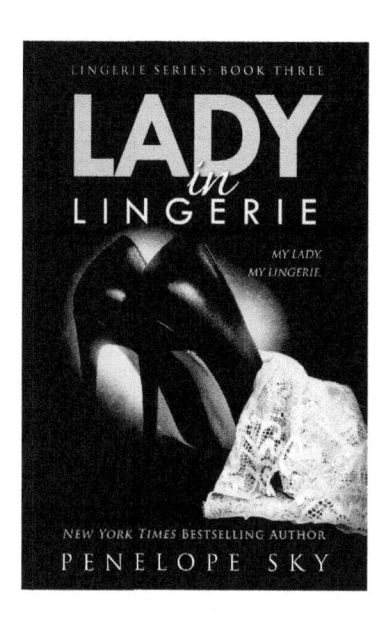

I refuse to let this woman have any power over me.

She's just my prisoner.

But once my Muse is in trouble, I'll do anything to save her.

Anything to protect her.

She was supposed to inspire me, please me.

She was never supposed to care about me.

Or make me care about her.

Order Now